The Dark Will End The Dark

The Dark Will End The Dark

Darrin Doyle

Tortoise Books
Chicago, IL

Published in the United States by Tortoise Books.

www.tortoisebooks.com

ISBN-10: 0986092215
ISBN-13: 978-0-9860922-1-3

Cover Design by Christopher Simons.

Tortoise Books Logo Copyright ©2012 by Tortoise Books. Original artwork by Rachele O'Hare.

The following stories have been previously published, some in slightly different form: "Head" in *BULL: Men's Fiction*; "Eyes," "Neck," and "Mouth" in *Toad*; "Hand" in *Blackbird*; "Penis" in *elimae*; "The Hiccup King" in *Snake Nation Review*; "Foot" in *Waccamaw Journal*; "Sores" in *Puerto del Sol*; "Happy Turkey Day" in *The Long Story*; "Ha-Ha, Shirt" in *Night Train*; "Tugboat to Traverse City" in *Alaska Quarterly Review*; and "Barney Hester" in *Harpur Palate*.

For Mom and Dad

But there, where western glooms are gathering
The dark will end the dark, if anything:
God slays Himself with every leaf that flies,
And hell is more than half of paradise.

— "Luke Havergal" by Edward Arlington Robinson

Table of Contents

Tugboat to Traverse City

The foghorn startled us all into silence. The women covered the children's ears. The men chuckled at the women. The women laughed at each other. The first mate stepped through the cabin door and apologized for the noise. Poised five feet above us, atop the tugboat's upper deck, he said the fog was as thick as oatmeal and that visibility was less than forty feet and likely to get worse. He assured everyone there was no danger. We would make it to Traverse City on time. With a wave and a smile and the delicate click of the latch, he disappeared behind his narrow metal door once again.

The other passengers – some two dozen in all, standing in groups of four, five, six – resumed talking. Three hours ago, at the five p.m. Ludington departure, with the sun bathing our faces and well-wishers waving *bon voyage* from the shoreline, we were strangers to one another. The tugboat had chugged pleasantly ahead as the land shrank in its wake. Each family, each group of friends, each couple, had stood in isolation along the rail, pointing at the glistening, undulating skin of the lake, commenting privately into each other's ears.

Then, as twilight fell and the fog grew out of the water, the crowd had congealed, with ease, into clusters of like-minded. The conversations centered on the weather.

From surrounding groups we caught the words "fog" and "foggy" and "dead." Monica rubbed her arms. Rick removed his flannel and draped it over her shoulders. Mitch continued his story about a baseball game he'd played in high school.

"So this guy whacks a long fly ball between right and center," he said, "and I'm hauling toward it, fog everywhere and getting thicker as I run. I can't see a thing in front of me. Just as I'm reaching out my mitt where I think the ball's going to land" – he acted out the gesture – "Wham!" he yelled. "I trip over something, a log I'm thinking, and down I go. Boom. The ball conks me on the back of the head. I'm out," he said, "cold."

Nobody responded. Deep down, we were waiting for the punch line. We needed humor. Our own fog was closing in. Our nervousness inspired us to recall, with internal pride, that this tugboat trip was *ours*. We owned it for as long as it took to reach Traverse City. We had paid for it with hard-earned money. We had refused the conventional passenger ship, the four-story *S. S. Badger* with its four-cylinder Skinner Unaflows and coal-fired steam engine, cushioned seats, overpriced cocktails, snack bar, and intercom voice chattering about the shoreline and the resident seagulls. We'd exchanged pampering for a chance to smell the lake, to feel the cold wind, to know hunger. We craved discomfort, or at least its beginnings. We craved danger, or at least its possibility.

Mitch continued. "I wake up two minutes later. Everyone's gathered around, staring down at me. They ask if I'm all right, the coach is wiggling his fingers, asks me how many he's holding up." He paused to light a cigarette, watch the smoke leave his mouth. "Come to find out I tripped over a naked man. A naked man in center field."

Monica's laughter triggered a bout of sneezing. We watched, amazed, as she sneezed eleven times, which made us laugh louder. Rebecca dug a packet of tissue from her purse and gave it to Monica. When our wave of hysteria settled, we looked around, teary-eyed. The other passengers were shooting unfriendly glances our way, suggesting that our level of fun was simply too high for this excursion. The solemnity of the fog's approach seemed to agree with them, but we didn't care.

"Strangest thing is," Mitch resumed, "I never actually *saw* the naked guy. Everybody else saw him – my buddies, my folks, the coach – said he had a long beard and shaggy hair – a textbook madman, I guess. He ran away as soon as they got close. They called the cops, and the cops searched the streets for hours. Never found him."

Gabriel spoke up. "So I guess your question is – if you trip over a naked man but never *see* the naked man, did you really trip over the naked man?"

Our conversation was interrupted by the foghorn. It rumbled our guts. We formed a row along the railing. We stood like the other passengers, facing the fog, studying it. We were surrounded. It had grown thicker, whiter. Wisps of it now touched the boat, delicate fingers breaking apart on the rusted railing. Mitch blew his cigarette smoke into the fog. Rebecca fanned the air, trying to clear a path, but only managing to stir the cloud before her. Soon we were bored of playing with the fog. We wanted it to go away.

The first mate emerged again, stooping through the cabin door, which closed behind him. He descended the four-runged rope ladder to the deck. He was built like a telephone pole. He fidgeted as if trying to find a comfortable angle to position his elbows.

"So what do you all think of this fog, huh?" He broadcasted a pleasant grin to his dependents.

"It sure is something," an old man said.

"How do you tell where you're going?" a woman asked.

"We were hoping *you* could tell us the way," the first mate said with a wink. A few people chuckled. One of them was the first mate.

"How much farther is it?" a different woman asked. Her tone was not cordial. She was the mother of a sick boy, maybe four or five years old, who slept at her feet.

In the yellow lantern light (we had paid for this crudity), visible only as a tangled mop of hair beneath a red wool blanket, the sick boy resembled a sea creature pulled from the bottom of the lake.

"Two hours in good weather," the first mate said, wiping a film of mist from his forehead with a handkerchief. "Maybe three or four tonight. We've just reached the tip of the pinky." He held forth the palm of his right hand, forming a crude Michigan map. "Traverse City, as you probably know, is in this area." He pointed to the inner tip of his ring finger. "We'll get you there as soon as humanly possible."

He tried to lift spirits by sharing an old lakefaring tale about a fur trader by the name of Gabe "Lurker" Ludlow, who in 1894 set off for Michigan from Chicago. Breaking the cardinal rule of long-distance water travel, Ludlow had attempted the journey alone. After eight hours he got caught in a terrible fog, worse even than tonight's. We all looked around and wondered how it could be worse.

"Back then," the first mate continued, "they didn't have high-tech guidance and radars and such." His chest inflated with pride. "Old Lurker can't find his way, ends up going due north, just like we are, right up the center of Lake Michigan, out here on 22,000 square miles of water! He's lost for three weeks, eats all his food, resorts to fishing. Eats perch raw right out of the lake."

The foghorn ripped a hole in the air. People visibly jumped. The sick boy woke in a panic and began crying for his mother, who knelt and caressed his head. The boy's face was the color of a marshmallow. He listlessly licked his cracked lips.

"So anyway, this story's got a happy ending," the first mate interjected. He was uncomfortable now; his elbows flapped impotently, like chicken wings. "Ludlow winds up on the shores of the U.P., all the way at the top of the lake, about where Manistique is nowadays. A nice Indian tribe takes him in, and a few weeks later Ludlow trades his watch for enough gold to live as a wealthy man. Never gets in another boat for the rest of his life. Ha ha. *Walks* back to Chicago. Ha ha."

The sick boy's mother announced that she needed flu medicine. The first mate chimed in eagerly, saying there was Dramamine in the cabin.

"You told me that an hour after we left," the mother said with measured annoyance, "and every hour since then. He needs *flu* medicine."

The child, who had been moaning, now began hyperventilating. Possibly he was delirious. In a thick voice he proclaimed to the sky that something bad was going to happen. He'd seen it in his dream. Something terrible was about to happen. His eyes were open, large and round, glazed over by the doppelganger alertness of a sleepwalker; he was certain of what he was saying but not a participant in our world as he said it. He tried to sit up, but his mother held him in place against the deck. Still breathing heavily, he closed his eyes. Soon, he was sleeping again.

Rick and Mitch circulated the flask. We took nips to fight the chill. We attracted the attention of a woman in a cinched trench coat, who sniffed in contempt before leaning to whisper this contempt into her husband's ear. The husband muttered a derisive comment that none of us could hear because the foghorn bellowed out another rib-shattering note. The lake beneath us swelled and dipped, which sent some people stumbling. Our little group, however, rallied together, drunk as we were, and grabbed each other's arms for balance. If one of us fell overboard, we were all going.

The lake swell ceased. We were stable again. While detaching, we looked at each other's arms, as if surprised that such frail things had kept us upright. The mother of the sick boy staggered to the railing and vomited into the water. At this unplanned prompt a cluster of well-wishers gathered around her. They formed a semicircle behind the queasy mother, reaching out to rub and pat her back. To us – to our group, who watched – the backdrop of the white, gathering wall of fog gave the deck the appearance of a stage set. From the touch-happy crowd of actors rose words like "sweetie" and "poor thing."

"People are too damn nosy," Mitch whispered. We had formed our own circle to pass the flask without scrutiny and protect our faces from the cold mist.

"Every little thing that happens…" Monica whispered.

"If you stop and tie your shoe, somebody's got to comment on it," Rick whispered.

"Why don't they get a life so they don't have to live everyone else's?" Rebecca whispered.

All these good points went unremarked upon because at that moment the sick boy rose from his sleep. He sat up beneath his blanket, eyes wide with alarm or horror. He stood, unsteadily. His hair resembled two atrophied hands pasted atop his head.

While the crowd focused on his mother, the boy shuffled toward the stern, cloaked regally by the floor-length red blanket he clasped at his neck. None of us said a word or moved to stop him. He shed his covering, climbed the rail, and dropped over the edge into the fog. We heard the thin splash.

We were frozen in place – arms crossed, hands pocketed, hands on hips, arms dangling, cigarettes dangling. We weren't sure what we'd seen was real, and didn't feel capable of commenting on it. Our common bond was that we'd read the pamphlets, read *all* the pamphlets, before choosing this particular trip. We had read so many pamphlets we could have written our own. We had explored every option meticulously. In the end, we were going from here to there, from A to B – that was all that mattered. Whatever happened on the journey was OK. We had cemented this agreement even though we'd never actually voiced it.

The only other witness to the event, a doll-sized girl with blond pigtails whose mouth was stained red by the cherry sucker in her mouth, apparently believed what she'd seen. She tugged at her father's coatsleeve and, in a tone we privately wished we hadn't lost, said, "The little boy went swimming."

Panic ensued. The mother rushed to the stern, calling the boy's name into the fog. She picked up his discarded blanket and cradled it. An alert gentleman climbed to the cabin and pounded furiously with his palm upon the door. The engine was cut, stopped dead. Silence fell over us like a heavy drape. Life preserver already in hand, the first mate sprang from the cabin. He commanded the passengers to keep calm and to "keep not talking." He said the only way to find the child was by listening. If we could hear him, he said, we could save him. With the new stillness we became more aware of the constant rise and fall of the Great Lake. It slapped the boat with its sloppy tongue. Nothing was stable. After a moment, the floorboards rumbled as the anchor was dropped.

"That anchor won't reach the bottom!" somebody yelled. "It's gotta be a thousand feet deep!" The rest of the crowd mumbled in agreement.

"What if he's under the boat?" another person added.

"He'll be dragged down with it!"

This prediction caused the mother to burst into a fresh round of hysterics.

The first mate aimed his beam over the lake. "Let's all just keep our heads," he said. His flashlight only succeeded in staining the fog yellow. Next he hurled the life preserver like an enormous Frisbee. The fog swallowed it. Everyone heard the life preserver's splash, but they couldn't see it. The first mate began pulling at the rope, one-handed, drawing the donut toward himself like a fisherman trolling for bass.

"He couldn't have gone far," the first mate said. "Can the boy swim?"

The mother said he could. He could swim. He could tread water and float on his back.

"Good. But we need to be silent," the first mate said firmly, still pulling the rope, staring wide-eyed into, and at, nothing. "We need to listen."

The crowd was skeptical. A slim, hard-faced man wearing a baseball cap stepped forward. "I'm going in after him," he announced. There was a collective gasp of admiration and disbelief. He removed his cap with a flourish and handed it to his wife. She clutched the battered hat proudly as her husband walked to the stern.

"Sir, you'll only endanger yourself," the first mate said. One hand directing the flashlight beam, the other guiding the preserver with the rope, he resembled an orchestra conductor. His face had broken into a sweat. He shone like a waxed quarter.

The admonishment seemed to break the capless man's resolve. He peered helplessly into the hypnotic whiteness. "Isn't there a goddamn lifeboat on this vessel?" he hissed. His voice broke against the wall of fog and fell into pieces on the deck. In the jaundiced, bandaged moonlight, his skin was the color of urine. His hair jutted and leaned, poking about. We imagined that on shore he was a GM executive or Amway superstar, but on the tugboat he might as well have been a homeless lunatic.

"If I. Don't. Get. Some. Quiet," the first mate hissed, "everyone on this vessel will face charges of impeding a rescue attempt."

A silence fell over the crowd. The mother's sobs became the only noise. Our group found a spot where we could sit, on the moist, hard deck. We arranged ourselves in an inward-facing circle, legs Indian-style. We wanted nothing to do with the present situation. Everybody else looked at us with bloodless faces.

"Now," the first mate said in a diplomatic voice, "If we could have everyone take a position along the railing and listen for the child's cries."

The passengers obeyed. All except us. Just as their decisions were being determined by forces beyond their control or understanding, so were ours. No one in our group said a word, but it was understood, without discussion, that our course of action during this nightmare would be to pass the flask and finish the trip we had chartered. They didn't need us.

Our decision was not popular. We were grumbled about, scolded with glares and head-shaking and flicked ashes. One woman leaned into Rick's ear and said we were shameful. None of us said a word in response.

"Where's the captain during all this?" Rebecca whispered, scratching a pebble out of its crater in her palm.

"I need to remind you people that this is a group effort," the first mate said to us. He had materialized, quite suddenly, out of the fog behind Rebecca's head. "We need total quiet." He disappeared again.

A few terrible minutes passed. The boy's mother was not the only one crying anymore. Choked sobs could be heard from all corners. Breathing for everyone was difficult; the fog was now among us, as a thin vapor settling into our laps. We listened.

"I hear him," the capless man announced. "I hear him out there."

There was nothing.

"Yes, I hear it too," the woman with the cinched trenchcoat whispered.

"I'm going in," insisted the capless man. "I can't stand here while a child drowns."

He flung off his shirt and leapt over the rail, like a kid hopping a fence to retrieve a baseball. His wife screamed. The men said, "Oh no, oh no," eyes darting, searching for someone to blame. The crowd swarmed to the rail where the man had vanished. Once there, they could do nothing else. The man's wife lost consciousness *and* her husband's cap as she tipped into the arms of a nearby gentleman, who immediately fanned her with his hand. It was a general frenzy.

We – our little group – were the eye of the storm. In our circle there was peace, although a nervous peace to be sure. We were tensed up, physically and mentally. We tried to be one with the boat, with the fog, in order to be separate from the horror, but it was not easy.

"I have to go in after him!" the first mate screamed. He handed the rope and flashlight to someone else (he didn't seem concerned with who took them – it was no one from our group). "He disobeyed me," the first mate said, "so now I have to put myself in danger." In a matter of seconds he'd removed his boots, flannel shirt, and socks. He stepped onto the rail. Before taking the plunge, he turned and offered his last words, words with such action-hero connotations that they would have been comical if not for the circumstance: "I'll be back." He jumped.

Couples clutched each other; prayers for deliverance were screamed into a sky that no one could see. Muted, broken sobs filled the void left by the dormant engine. The rabble sounded like a new breed of farm animal, braying for food.

Our group maintained its silence. What could be done? It was out of our hands. This was our consensus. We had a choice: We could be mastered by the horror, or we could refuse to give it a home in our hearts.

Two male passengers, buddies of the capless man, came to their own decision. They would go into the water together. They would rescue everyone, they said. They were excellent swimmers. They kissed their wives, linked arms with each other, and jumped over the rail. Everyone seemed appeased by this heroic gesture until, a moment later, the sick child's mother broke from the embrace of her appointed caretaker and bolted to the stern. With a shriek, she also dove into the fog.

The remaining passengers became quiet. The Great Lake sucked at the boat like a lozenge. Couples held hands. Families huddled. Then, one by one, each group walked to different areas of the railing. An exodus began. They believed that whatever lay beyond in the whiteness was better than this – this frigid, damp uncertainty, this loneliness, this hole left by their departed comrades. Some of them went quietly, without ceremony, stepping onto the railing and simply leaning into the fog until gravity had its way and pulled them overboard. Others went with dramatic flair, giving primal yells and plunging headlong into the mist. The couples stepped over the edge together, frightened but pleased to be hugging each other's bodies against the impending cold. There were tears, professions of love, nervous laughter, battle cries. The process took fewer than two minutes. Then everyone was gone.

We could hear them on all sides, splashing and wailing in the water. Our cigarettes were gone. A rawness crept into our throats. Many questions were on our minds, all focused on the captain: Where was he? Why was he letting this happen? Could he have saved them?

We stood. We helped each other to our feet. We brushed off each other's backsides, as friends do. Our faces were damp; our arms, too. The fog was being absorbed into our bodies, leaving its translucent residue on our surfaces. We turned to look up at the cabin, where the captain was presumably manning his post, though from our vantage point we could not verify this.

"Can anybody see him?" Monica asked, or it may have been Rebecca. The fog had turned us into shadows.

"Should we go up there?" Rick said.

"Or should we just stand here and wait?"

There was a short pause. We were all trying to think, as the sounds of death swelled around us.

"I vote for standing here," someone finally said.

Someone else agreed. Then someone else. We were all in agreement.

Foot

The man and woman didn't want him, but the baby came anyway. They didn't like the idea of abortion – so low-class – and once the boy was born, adoption wasn't possible: They loved his sour-smelling vomit and the way his lips pursed as he filled his diaper. The mommy held him up for photos. The daddy tossed him to the ceiling, laughing. The mommy quit her job at the advertisement firm, and the daddy worked sixty hours a week at the five-star restaurant where he was head chef so they could paint the nursery and get a nice oak crib and lots of educational toys.

When two years had passed, the boy, who knew all of his letters by sight and could sing three verses of "Mary Had a Little Lamb," began to consume strange objects. He ate dirt, soap, paper, and crayons. The pediatrician said it would pass. It got worse. Pencils, aluminum cans, staples, credit cards. Not a spoonful of the daddy's gourmet macaroni and cheese passed the boy's lips. After swallowing his own socks, though, the boy would announce: That's good! He'd giggle gleefully, not understanding why his parents stared so darkly at the table.

When the boy was three, the mommy awoke from a nap to find him gnawing on her leg. She screamed.

It became clear that the boy wanted to eat the mommy so badly that he couldn't concentrate on anything else. He stopped caring about letters and numbers. He stopped singing. He refused breakfast, lunch, and dinner. No glue piles, no bowls of buttons, no cardboard nuggets – none of the old meals satisfied him. He regressed linguistically, reverting to grunts, growls, and shrieks. He forgot his potty training and soiled his pants.

The mommy had a long talk with the daddy. This was a temporary regression, they decided, nothing to be alarmed about. A little boy needed to know that his mommy was still going to sacrifice for him as she had when he was a newborn. Once he believed his mommy was attending to all his needs, he would break free, move on, and become independent.

It was agreed: She would give up her right foot. Seeing his mommy limp through hallways and struggle to master short flights of stairs – all for him, only for him – would allow the boy to return to being smart and normal.

It took an entire afternoon (two sheets, ten towels, ruined), but the daddy severed the foot. The boy seemed happy for more than a week.

But truthfully, the boy had a difficult time. His jaw wasn't strong, and his teeth weren't sharp. The daddy had boiled it to soften the meat, even tenderized it with a mallet, but still, it was tough and fatty. The boy walked around the house carrying the foot like a toy. He kept it with him most hours of the day, even clutched it to his chest while he sat on the potty. It pleased him, but it was a source of frustration; he wanted to eat it. Now and then he bit a toe, wiggled his head, and tore off what he could. What he rent was impossible to swallow.

No, no, no, he said. He wiped his lips in disgust and licked at the air, trying to get the gristle from his mouth. He threw the foot on the floor and went to his bedroom to eat Play-Doh.

From her crutches, the mommy watched her boy and felt sad. Wasn't her foot good enough? Ten days had passed, she realized, and even if he did manage to get it into his mouth now, it wouldn't taste like her. It smelled rancid, and the skin was gray.

Where is the justice? the parents wondered as they stuffed the rotting appendage under a pile of towels on the bottom shelf of the linen closet.

They had grown to care about this boy, this boy they'd never wanted. They had made an enormous sacrifice for him, and he had treated it like a teddy bear. Or worse, actually, since he did manage to eat teddy bears on occasion.

The daddy was enraged and sickened. At first, he wanted to fuck and make a new baby, a baby with more forceful incisors. But while he discussed the dilemma with the mommy night after night, nodding solemnly and kissing the rim of his cognac glass, his mind wandered to his restaurant, where he envisioned his staff of robust, well-groomed youngsters, kids who respected and learned from him and who ate his culinary creations with gusto.

The daddy sipped his cognac and decided to simply ignore his son until the boy's shortcomings stopped inducing an unpleasant emotional reaction. Then he would be free. The process, he realized, was already underway.

The mommy, meanwhile, pitied the boy. He's just too young, she said. Maybe we need to wait a few years, until he's bigger.

And then cut off your other foot? the daddy said. So he can *not* eat that one, too? I don't think so.

The daddy had been raised by a firm-handed father, one who gave few second chances. The daddy didn't hesitate to apply the same tough love to his own child.

He convinced his wife to cut off the boy's foot in order to show the boy what a sacrifice felt like.

The boy didn't like it – hated it, in fact – when he woke up tied to the bed. Mommy went to work with the hacksaw. The boy screamed so violently that the daddy ran to the living room to crank *Aida* so the neighbors wouldn't hear.

In the end, the boy accepted it. He sat in the corner of his room, pouring puddles of motor oil into his hand and slurping them up. He hallucinated that he was a sick, beautiful bird, floating upward through the clouds, lighter than the sky, his abdomen buzzing and filled with love. When he opened his mouth, great waves rushed forth to blacken the world.

The mommy carried his small foot. It made her happy. She snuggled with it at night while the daddy was out playing poker or softball or cooking for VIPs. But when the mommy tried to eat the foot, it was too tough. Alone, she boiled it and tenderized it, to no avail. The daddy had been gone for six days.

Without any discussion – for she had no one to discuss it with – into the linen closet it went.

Maybe, the mommy thought, maybe when the boy's a little older...

The Hiccup King

Owen's coworker Clyde gave him the idea of seeking out the Hiccup King. They were seated on lawn chairs at the foot of the retractable loading ramp that extended like an enormous gray tongue from the semi bed to the grass. The Best Way Moving semi-trailer, angled across the front lawn, was one-third full of materials from Gary and Clarisse Eichler's four-bedroom house in Park Hills. Owen and Clyde unwrapped their takeout sandwiches. Clarisse Eichler appeared with a couple of ginger ales. The men thanked her, and she vanished wordlessly into the house, presumably to continue packing.

"She's a looker," Clyde said. He scrutinized his tuna sandwich before taking a prodigious bite.

Owen hiccupped before biting into his own sandwich, which was filled with processed turkey and loaded with mustard, which his ex-wife Tanya once called "the vinegar and oil of the middle class." He hiccupped a couple more times as he chewed. Business as usual.

"I'll assume when you hiccup it means you agree," Clyde said. This was one of his favorite jokes.

Owen hiccupped in reply. The men's eyes wandered casually over the suburban neighborhood. Everything glistened – the mailboxes, the recently tarred street, the wide and pristine lawns. Even the mailman's gray shorts seemed to glow. "Why would you ever leave a place like this?" Owen asked rhetorically.

"That white collar's too starchy for me," Clyde said. "I like moving the cubicle panels, not staring at them all day."

Owen mulled this over for a couple of hiccups. He'd always suspected that one of Tanya's reasons for leaving was his inability to afford a house in a neighborhood like this one. She'd never said it, but once she completed her B.A. in Sociology, followed by her master's degree, her sights turned to pottery catalogues, oak bookshelves, and operas.

"Mister Eichler probably got transferred," Clyde said. "Doubled his salary."

"Off to bigger and better things," Owen mused. "Chicago, Seattle. Anywhere but Kalamazoo."

"Hey, Chicago!" Clyde said. He sat up in his chair. "Reminds me. Have you read *Guinness*?"

Owen couldn't answer. He was holding his breath again. It was the only method he still attempted on a regular basis. He'd tried everything – drinking water from the far end of a glass, drinking water while doing a headstand, pondering what he'd eaten for breakfast the day before, having his friends leap out and startle him, meditating, swallowing spoons of sugar. The breath-holding was his final bastion of proactivity.

Clyde was used to it. He continued talking while Owen did an imitation of a statue. "This guy holds the world record. He lives near Chicago. Son of a bitch's had the hiccups for fifty years, so you shouldn't feel bad. His life's pretty normal, from what I can tell."

Owen expelled the air from his lungs. He allowed the inevitable hiccup to pass before he spoke. "Why should I care?"

"Because he's the Hiccup King!" Clyde yelled, suddenly passionate beyond all reason.

●●●

Owen lived alone in a one-bedroom house with a one-car garage, not far from a supermarket where he did his weekly shopping. Ground chuck, buns, frozen dinners, canned soup, bread, milk, cereal, beer: these were the regular purchases he diligently crossed off each new list. He cooked well enough to make a single man happy. Across the street there was a small, overgrown park. From his porch he could sip beer and view young mothers pushing strollers along the cracked sidewalk, shirtless boys throwing Frisbees, the mesh of shadows evolving on the grass during twilight.

He hiccupped every five to ten seconds. Most hiccups passed unheeded. They were as much a part of his aural landscape as the refrigerator hum or the chirping of birds. His body convulsed a bit, of course, at each one, but it wasn't the end of the world. Even sleep was possible. The needs of the body, he'd discovered, were far stronger than any external distraction: people slept on crowded subways; soldiers caught forty winks as bombs flashed in the distance; homeless folks snoozed in the eye of rush hour; people adrift in the ocean managed to hold their heads above water while slumbering. These were the cases the doctor cited during Owen's first examination, when he'd been told there was no way to determine when or how the hiccups would stop. That had been over a year ago.

If Owen thought about it, if he closed his eyes, he could pretend that this was only some vulgar dream. He could really go back into the peaceful, oblivious time when breathing was an unconscious function that existed wholly apart from, and unremarkable upon, his daily life.

But this retreat was too painful. Life in the present, however frustrating, was more satisfying than the past. He was a mover by trade, adept at moving on and starting fresh. He had a Class B Trucker's License, which allowed him to operate an 18-wheeler. He handled in-town moves and moves within a fifty mile radius of Kalamazoo. Ten to twelve hours a day, six days a week, he worked. Each night he slept in his own bed. This was a schedule that encouraged him to dwell in the Now.

His buddies didn't mind his handicap; they got used to it and cracked jokes that helped them all feel better. They drank beer and played euchre after work.

Owen's greatest talent was packing 36-foot trailers in the most spatially economical way that Best Way Moving had ever seen. For as long as he could remember he'd had a gift for arrangement. As a boy, he'd retreated into his room and assembled puzzles for hours. His father recruited Owen for the basement cleaning duties: Owen transformed the chaotic, unnavigable basement into a room that could accommodate a ping-pong table, a workbench, and a weightlifting bench, with room to spare.

The hiccups couldn't take these things away. But Owen had had a wife for four years, which the hiccups did take away.

She stuck it out for the first few months, but the sleepless nights, one disruptive *hic!* after another during her favorite television programs, during lovemaking, breakfast, lunch, dinner, family gatherings, funerals, weddings – it proved too much. She cited other reasons, of course, insisting that his "malady" (that was her term) was of no consequence. They simply didn't have much in common, she said. He was too content being a homebody. She wanted backyard shish-kebabs, dinner parties, and book clubs. He had no desire to travel, while she "ached" (again, her word) to see the Nile River. The romance was gone. She felt like an old maid at thirty. They'd gotten married too quickly, she said. A three-month courtship when they were in their twenties was not long enough, and now this "foolishness" (yes) had caught up with them. The time to split up was now, before children entered the scene and "put the final nail in the coffin."

Owen wasn't the begging type, so she slipped out of his life without even a spilled tear. Four years of his life – fizzle!

– out like a dud firecracker. "The hell with you then," he had told her as she walked out the door. He would forever wish he hadn't hiccupped on the word "hell."

That was eight months ago, and he didn't miss her. Not too much. He mostly missed the idea of her; he figured it would feel the same if one day his shadow detached itself and announced, "I'm leaving you, Owen."

It occurred to him that Tanya might have been right about their differences, and that his "malady" was just a poorly timed coincidence. In any case, he clung to the desperate hope that the hiccups would stop, somehow, as abruptly and inexplicably as they had started. "A quick inhalation of air caused by a spasm in the diaphragm and checked by the closure of the glottis" (according to the Merck Manual) certainly wasn't a debilitating defect, but as far as Owen could tell, no woman would want him in this condition. His only course of action was to wait.

His thoughts periodically returned to the Hiccup King. He envisioned an old, cotton-haired man leaning on a cane, his followers gathered at his feet to hear the blissful rhythm of his diaphragm. Of course he knew this wasn't true. Still, Owen loved the idea that there was someone out there who'd experienced the same peculiar and mystifying illness that wasn't really an illness. He longed for a comrade. He wanted company for his unremarkable misery.

One Sunday afternoon, after mowing the lawn, reading the paper, and drinking a cup of coffee, Owen drove to the bookstore for a copy of the most recent *Guinness Book of World Records*. It had been years since he'd read a book – *The Crucible*, in tenth grade – so the simple act of carrying it out of the store felt both nostalgic and invigorating. Fighting his compulsion to flip immediately to the Hiccup King's page, he decided to read the book from cover to cover. That way, when he came across the Hiccup King, it would be a wonderful surprise. He hadn't had a wonderful surprise in a long time.

•••

Periodically, he saw her. Once, he passed the window of a restaurant as she lunched with a woman he'd never met. Another time, he pulled up beside her at a stoplight. She puckered at her reflection in the rearview mirror, dabbing lipstick, oblivious to his presence. Two weeks later, at the crowded Secretary of State office, he observed her from across the room as she renewed her driver's license and he his hunting license. She never noticed him.

She didn't look any better or any worse. Her hair was still shoulder-length and light brown, the bangs hair-sprayed into a fashionable tangle. She wore the same knee-length skirts and earth-tone blouses with three-quarter-length sleeves that she'd worn for the five years he'd known her. Her lips still fell into a wry half-smile when she heard a joke. The incomplete smile indicated that the world could never impress her or catch her off-guard.

She was identical to the woman he'd married, and yet now she was a stranger. He knew her secrets – how her face behaved in the dead of sleep, her funny clenched teeth when she watched scary movies. He once helped her fish a detached wad of Q-tip out of her ear, settling her panic both during and after the ordeal. She didn't believe in the afterlife, but she believed in reincarnation. She bought generic pickles and butter but insisted on name-brand toilet paper.

None of these details, however, gave him any claim upon her. Her life was no longer his. Intimate knowledge of her served no purpose and would, over time, like the macaroni and cheese in his refrigerator, transform into something new, something unrecognizable and difficult to wash away.

•••

Owen wasn't sure he'd be able to find the man. But if they did meet, there was always the chance that they would become fast friends, brothers in bondage, and that they would go out for drinks, shoot pool at the local tavern, go pheasant hunting on Sunday mornings. Owen couldn't be certain of the outcome, but he knew he didn't want to rush anything, so although the drive would only take four hours, he planned for a longer trip.

A three-day weekend was easy to get: Owen hadn't missed a day of work in ten years. He was as regular as his spasming diaphragm. Packing, however, was tough. He spent twenty minutes in the garage, unearthing from the mountain of junk (nicely arranged junk, but junk nonetheless) his musty cream-colored duffel bag. It took another hour to wash and dry it. After that was accomplished, he had to think about what to bring.

It'd been years since he'd slept anywhere but this house. With mild surprise he realized it was the honeymoon in the Upper Peninsula. He summoned a vague list of what he'd packed for that trip: socks, underwear, condoms, shaving cream, a razor, toothpaste, a toothbrush. He didn't need condoms this time. Did he need towels? Soap? Long pants or shorts? T-shirts or button-down shirts? A tie? Camera? Sunglasses? In the end Noah's method was employed, and two of everything was forced into the bag until it was as swollen and tight as a pregnant woman's belly.

At just past dawn on Friday he hopped into his pickup and left Kalamazoo. Along both sides of the expressway the corrugated fields rolled. The breeze thundered through the open window. The white center lines zipped beneath him as if being violently inhaled by his truck. Strains of Air Supply poured out of the radio, successfully drowning out the sound of his hiccups. Life, he reflected, took shape in repetition: his heartbeat, his hiccups, the expressway lines, the tilled fields, the unceasing stream of radio songs, the sun climbing over the edge of the earth for another day of work. From a brown paper bag he removed an apple. He bit into it, and the juice dribbled down his chin.

His directions were vague. The name of the Hiccup King's town was Kankakee, Illinois. The Hiccup King's name was Irving Monroe. That's all he possessed in the way of information.

He'd read the *Guinness Book* at breakneck speed, finishing it in four days. When he'd reached the *Longest Bout of Hiccups*, he'd hardly been able to contain his excitement. Each word was a step closer to salvation. He was aware that there was only one chance to read these words for the first time, so he slowed to a torpid pace and mentally masticated syllables as if they were filet mignon. The facts were beautiful in their simplicity: Irving Monroe, a farmer, came down with the hiccups on Sunday, July 18th, 1950, at age twenty-nine – the same age as him! For the past fifty-seven years he had hiccupped every one-and-a-half seconds, but he managed to lead a normal life, fathering four children. He lived in Kankakee with his wife Elizabeth.

Every one-and-a-half seconds. Owen had read this with a guilty feeling of relief. Someone who was suffering four times as much as him. Suddenly his own life seemed four times better. He thought of all the peaceful, uninterrupted breaths he could still enjoy. Here he had been focusing only on the hiccups, rather than the spaces in between. Wasn't it within these spaces that he was living? Why should he only dwell on the anticipation of the next spasm? That was like waiting for a rainy day and then saying, "See! It always rains!" while ignoring the previous week of sunshine.

In an elated state he completed the journey. Directly off the expressway he cruised past truck stops, fast-food billboards, semis and convenience stores and roadside cafes. It was 1:00 P.M. when he crossed into Kankakee. It was an unremarkable town that resembled the outlying villages in Michigan, but Owen recognized a beauty here that he'd been blind to in his own state. The outstretched limbs of elm trees extended generously over the streets, children played hopscotch on sidewalks, sprinklers before old colonial houses waved their fans of water in greeting. The fire hydrants were yellow, as if stained by the sunshine.

He stopped at a gas station and filled up. He went in, paid, and asked the attendant if he could borrow a phone book, hiccupping as the words left his mouth.

"You need some water?" the attendant asked. He dropped the phone book onto the counter.

"I'm afraid that won't help," Owen said. Although he knew it by heart, he fished from the front pocket of his jeans the scrap of paper on which he'd scrawled Irving's name. "These are – *hic* – what you'd call chronic."

Adopting a clinical tone, the attendant, whose name tag read *Mitch*, said, "Plug your ears, plug your nose, close your eyes, and swallow three times. Worked for me for thirty-seven years."

Owen flipped through the white pages, nodding. If he had a nickel for every homespun remedy he'd heard over the last year and a half, he could almost afford the surgery. His heart did a jig in his chest when his index finger encountered *Irving R. Monroe 133243 County Road 28.*

"Wait a sec – " Mitch said, pausing to remove his chewing gum and dispose of it somewhere below the counter. He leaned forward and tilted his head to read. "You're looking for Irv Monroe! He's got the most chronic hiccups in the world!"

Owen laughed. "You know him?"

"He's the most famous person to come out of this town," Mitch said. "Pumped his gas for the last fifteen years, and my dad pumped his gas for twenty-five."

●●●

Owen followed Mitch's directions. Within twenty minutes, the Monroe house emerged on the horizon along County Road 28. Nothing in its appearance betrayed it as a farm, however, until Owen eased his truck onto the gravel drive and observed the tiny, dilapidated barn crouching among neck-high weeds just beyond the garage. The field beside the barn was equally overrun, so that only the faintest remnant of what might once have been tilled soil showed beneath the hairy crabgrass. A corroded Sunbird bearing a faded bumper sticker (*I'm a Farmer and I Vote*) sat facing the garage like a beaten dog begging to be let inside.

Owen cut the engine and took a deep breath. Stepping from the truck he strained his ears, half expecting to hear the King's hiccups ringing through the air like part of the natural surroundings. He walked to the front of the house and mounted the steps. He paused, reflecting. Inside was a man who for fifty-seven years had filled this house with an uncontrollable noise. To his loved ones, this man's hiccups had probably become like a heartbeat, another metronome of his life. How many sleepless nights – and terrible daylight moments, spent grasping for reasons – had passed within these walls? And yet to the cars drifting by on County Road 28, this was just another farm house, another obstruction of the horizon.

He knocked. A woman came to the door. She was as old as Owen's grandmother, with the same stooped posture and cloud-white hair. She jimmied the lock on the screen door and opened it a crack. There was an expansive kindness in her blue eyes that nearly broke Owen's heart.

"My name is Owen," he said. "I'm from Michigan. I'm looking for Irving Monroe."

"He's sleeping," she said. She gripped the collar of her white summer dress against the breeze. "If you're selling something, I'm afraid we don't have anything to spend."

Owen fought off the irrational desire to give her a hug while the woman allowed her gaze to wander beyond him, across the road and perhaps all the way to the horizon. She appeared to be dreaming, absorbing the sight like it was the first time she'd seen the outdoors in years. He could virtually see the images being swallowed by her pupils. Then Owen hiccupped. The old woman, as if shocked out of her meditation by a long-forgotten melody on the radio, leveled her eyes at him.

"You're not selling anything," she said.

"That's right," Owen said, feeling that his hiccup had in some way betrayed him. "I drove here to meet your husband – *hic* – excuse me. As you can tell, we have something in common." He paused as the words accumulated in his throat. "It would be a great help if I could meet him."

●●●

"Things aren't exactly hopping around here," she said. She set the teakettle onto the stove's eye. "The farm is pretty much kaput." She seated herself at the table across from Owen.

Her voice sounded loud in the silence of the kitchen. In fact there was no noise anywhere, except Owen's hiccups, which had continued with a terrible consistency, although he tried to stifle them. He wanted to get on with the business of meeting Irving but felt compelled to continue the conversation Mrs. Monroe had begun.

"What happened to the farm?"

"We're old!" she exclaimed, as if shocked that Owen hadn't noticed. She licked her lips in what Owen perceived as a nervous gesture, and then began pinching the tablecloth between her fingers. "Time steals from you. So gradually you hardly notice. This place is too big for the two of us. We're stubborn." She laughed, then adjusted her upper row of teeth, dislodging them and repositioning them with her tongue, accompanied by a wet suction sound.

A few minutes later, the water boiled. Mrs. Monroe served tea. Owen thanked her. There was a weak cough from an adjoining room.

"That's Irving," Mrs. Monroe said. She sipped her tea and apparently forgot about it.

A long silence followed, broken only by Owen's hiccups. "Mrs. Monroe," he whispered, "I've had the hiccups for almost two years now." He searched her face for a reaction but got none. She wasn't even looking at him. "It pretty much ruined my – *hic* – marriage. It's the kind of thing that can consume a person, as I'm sure – *hic* – you know. I read about your husband. The Gui – *hic* – ness Book. It made me happy to hear there was someone with the same problem – *hic* – as me." Owen stared into the calm brown oblivion of his tea. "I don't know what I need, exactly. I just want to talk to your husband. *Hic*. Then I'll get out of your way."

Mrs. Monroe finally summoned the necessary courage – or energy, or whatever was turning those cogs – and went to the bedroom. She told Owen to wait "a piece." He fidgeted in his chair. He walked to the kitchen sink.

On the window ledge stood a collection of salt and pepper shakers: miniature corncobs, light bulbs, kittens, apples, oranges, bars of soap. Owen's gaze drifted over the counters, encountering one pair after another, hundreds, perhaps thousands more. Airplanes, automobiles, Coca-Cola cans, pumpkins, an apple pie with a slice removed, a farmer and his wife, TV sets, dice, slot machines, pancake stacks, work boots, robots, lemons, tubas, scuba divers, plump French chefs. On the bureau a few feet away, the telephone was engulfed by salt and pepper shakers. A shelf installed around the periphery of the room, two feet beneath the ceiling, was filled. In the living room, the television and the bookshelf crawled with shakers. It was a true infestation.

Mrs. Monroe peeked out of the bedroom. "You can talk to him now," she said, flashing her dentures. "Please keep it short."

The room was dark and filthy. Clothing stood ankle-deep on the floor. Owen stepped through the mess, following Mrs. Monroe. A torn shade drawn over the sole window allowed a narrow band of sunlight into the room, but it didn't illuminate anything – the light lay across the center of the bed as if trying to divide this world from the next.

Irving Monroe wasn't more than a slight disturbance beneath a blanket. Owen stood at the side of the bed and tried to find a face in the darkness. He heard a soft hiccup. It fluttered into the air and vanished, like a wisp of ember.

"Elizabeth says you got what I got," said a tired, thin voice that had no apparent source.

Owen hiccupped, as if to prove it. The old man hiccupped. Owen hiccupped again. The old man let off another one. It went on this way for a few seconds, as if the two men were communicating in a primitive language. Elizabeth, standing near the window, started to cry.

"She always does this – *hic* – when I have a guest," Irving said. Then to his wife, "Why don't you – *hic* – wait out in the – *hic* – kitchen."

Elizabeth obliged. The bedroom was stiflingly hot. The pungent smell of ointment and unwashed flesh had replaced the oxygen. Irving's breaths rattled his insides audibly. He was dying; this was obvious to Owen.

"I needed to see you," Owen said. "Sometimes I think I'm losing my mind – *hic* – with this. It's too much, but at the same time, it's nothing."

Hic. "How long've you been going?" Irving said.

"Almost two years."

"And what – *hic* – seems to be the problem?"

There was no irony, no humor, in his tone. Owen contemplated the question. Was he looking for a list of physical symptoms? A catalogue of the inconveniences? An account of his mental anguish?

The Hiccup King let out a broken laugh from deep inside. "You want my advice? Go for the record!" His volume was unsettling. "Only fifty-five years left." In his throat, a chunk of phlegm dislodged with a crack.

Shortly after Irving's laughter faded, he fell asleep. Owen leaned in, listening. He waited for a minute. He didn't hear any hiccups other than his own.

●●●

Elizabeth escorted him to his truck. Her face was red from crying. It hadn't taken much prompting to get her to confess the truth. Irving had caught the hiccups, just like the Record Book said, back in 1948. Irving tried everything, went to doctors, specialists, but they kept going. Some folks tried to help, but even more wanted to come and stare, to get a glimpse of the man with the never-ending hiccups. The press caught hold of it, and Irving became a local celebrity. He and Elizabeth were invited to parties and black-tie dinners up in Chicago, all because of his hiccups.

Then one day, eighteen months later, the hiccups stopped. Just like that. Irving wasn't happy about it. He was depressed. He sat around for weeks, doing nothing, and then he figured, "Why not keep going?" What did he have to lose? He could live normally at home, but when people visited or when he went out in public, he would fake it. So that's what he did for half a century. And the day the people from *Guinness* came to the farm to validate the record – that day was the best of Irving's life.

"Please don't tell anyone," Elizabeth said as Owen climbed into his truck. "Maybe the record's really yours, huh? Maybe you can be proud."

●●●

He still saw her. Even after he returned from Kankakee, Tanya was there. And why wouldn't she be? On the drive home he'd convinced himself that she would be gone, out of the country, satisfying her "ache" in some third-world jungle. But there she was, as she always was and would be, poised on the periphery of his life – at the bank, coffee shop, gas station, post office – not every day, not every other day, not even weekly, but often enough for each occurrence to sustain itself in his mind until replaced by the next one. She never noticed Owen, never sensed his presence. He even tried to hiccup as loudly as possible, to see if it would trigger a reaction. It never did.

Clyde continued to prod him about the Hiccup King. "You ought to check him out," he said, as they maneuvered a bookshelf down a flight of stairs. "There'll never be another one like him." A corner of the bookshelf dug into the wall.

Owen changed the subject. He would never talk about Kankakee. It was his alone.

●●●

A few months later, Clyde got married and moved to Indiana. Owen said goodbye to his friend and was promoted to dispatch manager. New management bought the company, new workers came and went, and for a while the only consistent thing about Best Way Moving was Owen's hiccups. With the money from his promotion, he reroofed his house and doubled the size of his garage.

On one occasion, he met Tanya for coffee. With her master's degree, she'd landed a job as a field researcher for a local pharmaceutical firm. Her travelling, which she'd so vocally craved, had thus far amounted to a long weekend in Minneapolis with her dentist, who, it turned out, was married. In Owen's eyes, Tanya was physically more beautiful than ever, but whatever had once bound them as husband and wife had been eroded by time into a few inside jokes, a few shared memories. She looked upon Owen with wistfulness whenever he hiccupped. They shook hands and parted as friends.

One morning, Owen awoke. He took a shower, shaved, and brushed his teeth. As he applied his deodorant, he noticed something was missing. His hiccups were gone. Anxiously, he hunched over his morning paper, sipping his Sanka, expecting at any moment that they would descend upon him again like birds of prey. But they didn't. Without giving himself time to think about it, he called in sick to work.

He felt like celebrating but had no one to celebrate with. He cracked a root beer and went to the calendar to calculate how long they had lasted: two years, eight months, and eleven days. His prison term was over. Deep down in his gut, somewhere near his diaphragm, he knew that he was free.

•••

In time, Owen forgot. His hiccups became an intangible thing: like a dream; like his childhood; like his marriage. It amazed him how quickly it happened. It was like stepping out of one car and getting into another. He met a woman named Connie at a bowling alley, and after six months of dating they married. They lived together in the one-bedroom house across the street from the overgrown park with the cracked sidewalks. She worked part-time at the local greenhouse. On weekends, she dug up the backyard into a serviceable garden. She got pregnant and gave birth to a girl, who they named Lisa. Using his great powers of rearranging, Owen transformed the den into a nursery and the basement into a den.

When Owen and Connie's baby was born, Clyde and his wife came to Michigan for a visit. After dinner, the women hung drapes in the nursery as Owen and Clyde relaxed in front of the television. Lisa slept in a portable crib beside the couch. The men sipped beer, recalling their days at Best Way until something caught Clyde's attention.

"Hey!" he yelled, nearly upsetting the bag of chips in his lap. "Shut up! That's the guy!"

Owen used the remote to turn up the volume. A picture came on the screen, a black and white photo of a man in overalls. The reporter said it was Irving Monroe.

"He's the Hiccup King!" Clyde hollered. The baby began crying. "Now I guess he's dead."

He had died of something, some ailment or condition that went unheard beneath Clyde's yelling. Once Clyde was silent, Owen listened to the story. Mr. Monroe had come down with the hiccups on July 18th, 1950, and continued to hiccup once every 1½ seconds until he passed away. He had been immortalized in the *Guinness Book of World Records*. He was survived by wife Elizabeth and four children. Elizabeth described Irving as an "unflappable man" and "a wonderful husband and father who never let hiccups get in the way of success." His record, according to the reporter, was unlikely to ever be broken.

Penis

The man squeezes into a space between refrigerator and wall. Breathing feels asthmatic. Heat climbs everything.

The moon offers a square of light. Or not, in truth, a square. Upon the linoleum it resembles distended farmland viewed from a plane.

The man is forty and wants to live old. This night she'll kill me, he knows. A metallic scream from the attached garage scores his eardrums. She's out there, probably, his wife – her claws in violation of codes, contracts, decency – and his Mercedes, his reward for years in medical sales.

The man visualizes a fingernailed car door and finds to his surprise that he doesn't care. Bald radials, oil-burning engine, eroded brake pads – is he describing himself? He hasn't driven the Mercedes in months. He hasn't showered. His life has crumbled and his wife did the damage but he can't prove it and now he no longer cares.

Let her. He slides from the cramped hiding spot, gathers a lungful, and faces the door. In fact, *please* destroy my car, he shouts. It has brought nothing but misery.

He feels committed; he has changed his life just now.

The car-scratch ceases. He hears the pulse of crickets, a thousand tiny policemen blowing whistles.

How easily she succumbs to reverse psychology. His lungs unblock. He feels springy in Kansas. This is his house, his life! Fightless surrender won't happen. He resolves.

A gentle tap sounds at the door.

It's just like her to change tack. Well, I can change, too.

The man pulls down his pants and shorts. He scuffles, counter-bound. The door is locked – a strong bolt – but she has a key, and in moments or seconds she'll be through, won't she? And then what?

She knocks a second time. Impatient. Or so it seems. He wonders how many times he has been wrong about her, starting when. Any number would be impossibly low or high. He draws the carving knife from the block and thumb-checks its sharpness.

On the third knock, his other hand gathers his bundle, precious. Blade raised. Ready. Ready for sacrifice, ready for blood.

Deadbolt clicks. Knob turns.

The man's father steps inside, towering in a black suit. Jacket sleeves cover him to the knuckles. His face is crabmeat. His pomaded hair gives back the moonlight.

I nicked your car, says the father, just before he sees: the bare legs, the knife, the cupped hand. His fatherly eyes, grim and familiar, issue a challenge. You're in a kitchen, for Pete's sake.

I was expecting someone else, the man says. He glances about for a place to set the knife. In the damned kitchen both counters reside beyond arm's length.

The moment is death and close enough. Because how can he move without toppling? And what kind of man falls nude while his father stands watching?

Head

The husband's head stopped.

No trauma. No pain. No warning. In the middle of explaining to a woman from Duluth that her policy did not cover any act of God involving water, and therefore, regrettably, she would not receive Prime Way compensation, the husband's words were snuffed out like a candle under a glass.

He fell into blackness. All sound sucked away.

He was aware of the physical world, but from a distance, as if he had plunged into a deep hole. He no longer conceived of either his hand or the receiver; he only sensed, wordlessly, that a distant part of himself stood in contact with something not of himself that could be used for destruction.

On the surface, he roared into violence.

Two colleagues subdued the husband when he began hitting his computer monitor with the phone. While they wrestled him to the floor, the men noticed how his head drooped like a flower with a broken stem. Saliva spilled from his mouth. They wondered if he was dying, and each privately imagined commandeering his vacated cubicle.

The coworkers resented the husband, not only because his desk stood nearest the restroom. He never took sick days. He was always on time. For more than ten years, he'd skipped the Monday doughnuts. He was supremely disciplined or supremely spineless. Either way, they hated him for making them slobs by comparison.

Paramedics rushed the husband to the hospital. Neurologists applied non-invasive tests for two hours, after which they declared his head "no longer viable."

Bedside, they pronounced the diagnosis. The patient didn't hear.

Engulfed in blackness, he only felt a queasy, off-pitch drone signaling that his essence was motionless, rootless, and cosmically out-of-touch.

He bucked and flailed and tore at the doctors' shirts.

Burly staffers situated the husband under heavy straps and inserted a pillow behind his head. The nurses frowned at him. "Such a tragedy," one said. "Still got most of his hair," said the other. The first rubbed her finger and thumb together. She clucked her tongue at the Rolex on his bedside table. "You can't take it with you," the other one agreed.

●●●

The hospital notified the wife, who left her yoga class to be with him. She stroked the husband's chest and held his hand. He lay with his face toward her, his blue eyes wooden. It was unnerving, this deserted stare. His bloodless cheeks appeared deflated, or perhaps this was an effect of the milky light filtering through the curtains.

It had been weeks, the wife realized, since she'd bothered to really see him. He'd become a collection of parts and impressions: a mouth, an arm, dirty socks, Barbasol. Studying him now, he scarcely resembled the man she'd married. This thing on the bed was a sculptor's rendition, a mannequin.

The lining of the wife's skirt caused her knees to itch. A chill rode her body. The diagnosis made no sense. A dead head? Was this a joke?

She thought she should get a second opinion. But if the second doctor said it was just a concussion, wouldn't she automatically believe it? It was human nature to cling to the more palatable answer. In the end, wouldn't the palatable diagnosis turn out to be wrong? And wouldn't the husband die? And wouldn't she be hobbled by guilt forever? And wouldn't their daughter feel resentful? And years later, becoming a mother herself, wouldn't the daughter resent her own daughter for making *her* feel guilty about having resented her mother?

Even under normal circumstances, such questions often plagued the wife. She dreaded mistakes, although normally her fears involved buying off-brand toilet paper, or visiting the salon when she'd just read about an Alabama woman who'd contracted leprosy during a pedicure.

Her hippie parents had raised her to be skeptical of authority figures, and even though the wife wasn't a hippie and in fact resented her parents' knee-jerk anti-establishmentarianism and New Age spirituality, she'd always embraced the inquisitive impulse. Until now. Lately, questioning felt like a euphemism for self-doubt.

She decided not to get a second opinion.

The husband stared. His chest rose and fell.

Gazing into his lusterless eyes, she felt certain that she loved him. Yes, he had his flaws: his collection of internet porn; his unwillingness to discipline their teenage daughter; his obsession with the Vietnam War (which had claimed his father's life); his middle-age flab; his foot fungus; his devotion to Prime Way.

Why go on? Nobody was perfect. People were more than lists, right? What was she supposed to do? Line up the good over here, the bad over there, and see which side was longer? Ridiculous.

Choking on the stench of isopropyl alcohol, the wife craved a cigarette. The urge swept through her. She pictured herself lighting one and pulling a long drag – her first in, what, two decades? She needed the distraction.

"You're the experts," she said to the neurologists by the window. For ten minutes they'd been studying her from behind clipboards. "But if his head is," she struggled for the right word, "a *vegetable*, then why is he breathing? Why do his hands move?"

The younger doctor chuckled. "No one said *vegetable*. We said *no longer viable.*"

"But why is his body moving?"

"Ever seen a chicken without a head?" the young doctor asked. "It has all kinds of moves. In Ohio, 1993, a farmer chopped off a chicken's head. But the chicken survived. They stuffed bits of apple into its neckhole for forty days before it died."

"Your husband's condition is unusual, but not unheard of," the older doctor interjected. "There was a case in Mexico in the '70s. Or was it Beirut in the '80s?" He looked to his colleague, who pursed his lips and said nothing. "The good news is that your husband's motor functions are completely normal. He can stand, walk, run. He could tap dance on a tennis court if he was into that sort of thing. Theoretically, of course. I mean he's physically *capable* of it. Whether or not he does it, that's another issue, and I wouldn't get your hopes up. His lungs are drawing air, however, so he won't die. Eating isn't a problem, as he is still able to swallow liquids. But he can't chew. Nor can he be trained to chew. In many ways, however, he's still the man you married."

The young doctor interrupted: "Think of the head as just another appendage. A glorified arm."

The wife was about to say she didn't marry him for conversations with his arm, but a nurse sidled up to the other side of the bed and inserted a tube between the husband's lips. By squeezing a translucent sack, the nurse sent clay-colored paste into his throat. The husband's throat convulsed. Now and then she repositioned his face so the tube remained intact.

The wife couldn't stop picturing her husband doing a theoretical tap dance on a tennis court. "Don't you mean his *brain* isn't viable?" she said.

"We said head, we mean head," the young doctor answered. "Squeeze his cheek. Go on."

When the wife hesitated, the young doctor reached across her and administered an aggressive pinch. The husband's skin reddened, but he gave no response.

"The entire head is without feeling," he continued. "Not only the brain."

"The bigger question is this," the gray-haired doctor interrupted. "Do you want to leave the head intact?"

"He no longer needs it." The young doctor's tone suggested they were discussing the fate of a shabby baseball cap.

The wife returned the young doctor's gaze without feeling. She wanted him to witness, displayed on her own face, his profound insignificance. He was aware of his good looks, which annoyed her. Early thirties, she guessed, bleached teeth, a forehead tall as a billboard. A hotshot. Always got what he wanted. Graduated med school by twenty-two. Swarthy eyebrows the color of her husband's shoulder mole. Every click of his pen was an attitude.

The older doctor cleared his throat. "His head will become unsightly in the coming weeks," he said, fingering his wattle in a way that made the wife sad. "It's not necrotic yet, but blood flow has dramatically decreased. All that bobbing will stress the neck."

The young doctor described the amputation procedure. His accent was Greek – or Turkish? – his hands fluttering like birds as he spoke. Distracted by his enthusiastic pantomime, the wife caught only random phrases: "Fourth and fifth vertebrae," "donate to science," "purely cosmetic," "minimal scarring, easily hidden."

The young doctor slid a brochure into her fist. His complicated odor filled her nose. She said she would think about it.

●●●

The husband was discharged the next day.

At home, he demonstrated the ability to walk, grab, hold, and kick. He could push buttons on the remote, but he did so without purpose and pressed so forcefully that the plastic cracked. He voided his bowels wherever it happened, in part because he couldn't see, hear, or speak. He didn't seem to understand where, or what, he was, or even what a "what" or "where" was. He was a 224-pound pastrami sandwich.

●●●

"Can he think?" the wife had asked, while signing the release form. "Will he know me or our daughter? Will it help if I sing our wedding song? Or read passages from *The Greatest Generation*?"

"All doubtful," the young doctor said with a lusty smile, his pheromones filling a balloon between them, jostling her, bumping her. "You need a brain for those things. His brain is literally a pile of macaroni." He pointed to the MRI results while sliding a hand around her waist, giving a squeeze.

"I see what you mean," the wife said. Her face heated. The neurologist was an idiot; he used "literally" in literally the wrong way. He was an inch shorter, fifteen years younger. And she wasn't pushing him away.

●●●

Now she was home with her husband, who staggered, lurched, and bulldozed. He toppled lamps and collided with walls. She placed a bottle of beer into his hand – his favorite, St. Pauli Girl. He poured it on his lap and the rest of the world. He'd become a collection of reflexes, a machine. Before, he'd at least been a machine that could get drunk and dress itself.

His destructiveness transcended slapstick. Objects in his reach became crushed or weapons or both. Hummel figurines inherited from his mother exploded against the ceiling. Burst bananas spilled their guts over his fingers. His null stare never changed. His head was a bell clapper.

The wife retreated to a corner, transfixed. The slamming of her heart wasn't from fear. She knew, without any evidence that she could articulate, that her husband wouldn't hurt her. What she felt was awe. He was more energetic than she'd ever seen. He'd never been violent. All of his successes had come from a measured persistence and lapdog charm he wasn't even aware he possessed.

She kept thinking of the doctor's words: "In many ways, he's still the man you married."

She couldn't decide if this was true. Yes, he was still distant and uncommunicative. Yes, he didn't ask about her day or help with the dishes.

But now he had a fire inside. His passion was directionless, untamed, and on display. He wasn't siphoning himself into that goddamn Vietnam book, hunched over a keyboard in the dark.

And now he liked to be touched. Her hand on his knee, fingertip on his back, toe on his foot – any contact – and he settled. He stilled.

The husband had never stilled. He'd worked eleven-hour days, taken meals in front of the TV, played on the computer until midnight, read in bed until she forced him to kill the lamp. While asleep, he even mumbled about the NFL draft, and revision deadlines for debris removal clauses.

●●●

The wife tied the husband to the recliner with nylon rope. This was in order to cook, go to bed, take a shower, drive their 15-year-old to school, and so on.

The wife brought the daughter into the living room so she could see the husband struggling against his restraints. The wife only wanted to frighten the daughter a little. She wanted the daughter to understand that this was serious.

The daughter frowned at her fingernails and scrolled through her text messages. She hadn't been close to her father, emotionally, since he had taught her to fly a kite. So while the sight of his limp head was upsetting (the daughter's eyes glistened with tears...unless...was she high?) she apparently viewed the current medical trauma as an adult issue that had nothing to do with her.

"I get it, Mom. It's serious. *Life* is serious. I'm bloated, and I've got a huge Econ test I haven't studied for."

"Okay. So this is *more* serious. Take your serious and multiply it. Here. Here's a calculator. Multiply it."

In the following days, the daughter's attitude worsened. "You say it's tragic," she said over Quaker Oats, "but he's alive, isn't he?" She nodded at the husband, who was duct-taped to the kitchen chair. "I needed to be fed when I was a baby. Was I a *medical emergency*? God, Mom."

The daughter continued, her words rapid-fire (didn't meth do that to a person?) "In fact, he's more present now than ever. And don't you want to be a part of it? Don't you want to repay his kindness – all those years he slaved so you could paint nude models and do Pilates? He's *here*. Isn't this what you've wanted?"

The outburst caught the wife off-guard. The daughter's normal mode of communication consisted of sighs and sardonic chortles. The wife whipped up a succinct response: "It's not your place to tell me what I want. Let's not forget who's boss."

The daughter acted as if she hadn't heard. "Isn't this so-called 'crisis' actually a miracle? This isn't a health emergency, Mom. It's a karmic imperative."

The wife needed to disguise the panic that was brewing inside her. "Where did you hear that phrase?"

The daughter stood and pointed at the husband. "Karmic imperative, Mom. To balance the cosmic scales and show this man we will not allow him to escape this mortal coil without achieving true intimacy!"

The wife leaned over the sink, staring into the drain. Her daughter's words echoed as a sick chorus – *karma, cosmic scales, intimacy*. It was true, then. Despite the wife's best efforts to live a disciplined, materialistic existence (a life of goals, competition, and earning, where goods weren't a badge of greed but a badge of merit that showed you were *alive,* you *desired*, you were self-sufficient and – God forbid – evolved), the granola gene had passed through her and into the child. The wife blamed herself. Who else could she blame? Her parents had been dead for ten years.

Maybe this was the husband's doing. All that anti-war talk since the daughter was small. All those PBS specials and History Channel documentaries. The husband never said specifically that war was wrong. But the daughter had a brain. She'd seen the footage. The brutality, the bombing, the burning. She knew that her father's father had never returned from his second tour of duty.

And for all of his insurance acumen, the husband had never been a go-getter. He had served Prime Way for years and was never offered the Regional Director position. He accepted his annual 2.5% raise and didn't request more. This house – this life – was adequate, but it could have been nicer. The Websters had a Jacuzzi. The Clemenses had a 78-inch plasma and a landscaper.

The wife decided to take action.

She turned from the sink and faced her daughter. "I have a surprise. Today you can drive yourself to school in the new Cherokee."

"That's Dad's car."

"He's not going to need it."

"I don't have a license."

"A permit's the same damn thing. And here's a hundred bucks. Get yourself another tattoo."

●●●

Prime Way offered generous disability, so the family was covered for a year – dependent, of course, on the wife's ability to convince HR over the telephone that the husband would return to work.

The HR representative was a stickler. She requested to speak with a member of the medical staff to confirm the non-chronic nature of the husband's condition.

It wasn't difficult to find the young doctor.

"It's about time," he laughed over the phone. His presumptuousness both irked and excited the wife. He was challenging her beliefs, taunting her values.

What beliefs? What values? The wife didn't know. But he was taunting *something*, and it pleased her.

He had remained in her thoughts for the past two weeks. She'd begun to make him more beautiful than in real life – she gave him vital lashes; soft, hirsute hands; burnt-almond eyes aflame with need and compassion.

She envisioned her husband wearing the same gaze – the idea made her giggle at the counter while whirring chuck for his dinner. Her husband was one of those rare people who'd been born satisfied, and every day from infancy had rearranged itself to fulfill his birthright. He had never needed anyone. He was disgustingly self-reliant. He even took the central trauma of his life – his father's death in Vietnam – and turned it into a project, a book he would never complete because it was the *process*, he said, that healed him.

The paste in the blender reminded her of dog food.

That evening, at the wife's urging, the daughter went to the Clemenses to babysit. The doctor parked his black Audi in the driveway. The wife spent the evening with him. Every action of the young neurologist both exceeded and disappointed her expectations.

He cracked jokes. She didn't understand the punch lines. He dressed impeccably, looking rigid and striking in his gray wool jacket and mauve turtleneck. A smear of shaving cream decorated his Adam's apple. She ordered Chinese. He ate with a fork and burped into his hand. He selected a CD of classical waltzes, then pushed aside the coffee table and took her into his arms. His heel crushed her bare toes. After dancing, they drank merlot. She tickled him; he wasn't ticklish. They discussed movies and vegetables, neither of which he truly understood. He kissed her on the mouth for two minutes, and then, catching his breath, asked, "Where's your husband, by the way?"

"In the closet."

"May I see?" His wine-stained lips were blood clots.

They dragged the husband to the center of the living room. His arms were crossed over his chest, bound like his ankles. His eyes were open.

"Fascinating." With a pen light from his jacket pocket, the young doctor illuminated the husband's eyes. "No response. And yet..." he paused before rearing back and punching the husband in the groin. "Watch." The husband convulsed; he writhed and strained; tendons bulged in his neck.

The wife was too stunned to speak. She smelled excrement. The husband had flooded his diapers.

"My point," said the young doctor, appearing not to notice the wife's tears, "is that we have always thought that cognitive function was necessary for pain. Or pleasure." He found the wife's hand and stroked it like a gerbil. He brought her close and embraced her, kissing her neck. "Perhaps we, too, can experience pleasure without our heads."

•••

For three months, flowers and cards arrived. Her husband was generally well-liked, but not specifically. The cards contained no personal messages. Visitors were rare: a coworker; the daughter's art teacher; an uncle; a cousin. The husband's only immediate family was his brother, a corporate attorney who flew from Chicago on his own twin-engine with wife and four young sons in tow.

The brother insisted on untying the husband.

"Let me wrestle him," he said to the wife. He rolled up his shirtsleeves. "It'll jar his memory. We horsed around constantly when we were kids."

The match ended with the husband fracturing the brother's wrist. More damage would have been done if the eleven-year-old nephew hadn't leaped onto the husband's back and compelled him into a china hutch. The husband's right eyebrow was lacerated; an expensive vase shattered. The brother and his wife threatened legal action while walking out the door.

That evening, the young doctor peeled off the bandage to check the husband's eyebrow.

"I trust you were able to stop the bleeding," he asked.

The wife, on the couch, was attempting to repair the vase. She took a gulp of wine. "There was barely any blood. Do you have to do that while I'm sitting here?"

The young doctor was stitching the husband with needle and thread. The husband wriggled on the carpet. His hands were turning purple. "Hold still, bucko," the young doctor said. Then, to the wife: "Come here and touch him so he stops moving."

"You're cutting off his circulation," the wife said. "I keep telling you, you tie him too tight. That's why he struggles. Do you have any heavy-duty medical glue at St. Mary's?"

"For your husband?"

"For the vase."

"Actually, yes. There's an epoxy for broken skulls. Strong stuff. I'll bring home a tube. I don't know why I didn't think of that!" He winked at her.

Home, he was calling it. Third time this week. The wife wasn't sure how to feel. Lately, she was having trouble knowing how to feel about many things: the laundry; her new deluxe mop head; her daughter's ennui; the stubborn cucumbers. The world was a soup, something creamed, through which she waded each day. She socked her husband's feet in the mornings and brushed his teeth at night. She swabbed him, shaved him, and changed his Depends. The young doctor worked eighty hours a week, slept with her when he could, and used their treadmill. The wife had taken up smoking. She rarely changed out of her sweat suit. Yoga, birdwatching, friends – these parts of her life had faded into memory.

"Oh, nuts," the young doctor said.

The wife glanced up from the shards in her lap.

The young doctor, cross-legged on the carpet, held forth his needle, which bore a skewered eyeball. The optic nerve and blood vessels dangled.

"It popped right out," the young doctor said.

"You did it on purpose. Are you pretending you didn't?"

"Let me get this straight. I took out his eyeball...why?"

"Don't patronize me. I'm not one of your chesty interns. I don't have lip gloss on my nipples, okay?"

"You worry me."

"Get in line."

"I don't understand."

"It means I worry *myself*. I thought you were a native speaker. You don't get the euphemisms, do you?"

"I never said native speaker. I said persuasive speaker."

"Did you lie about your past? From Cleveland, born and raised?"

"I can't be sure of what I said. I'm not a native speaker."

"Are you trying to bilk me out of my money? I'll burn down this house before anybody like you gets rich off it. He designed this house, okay?" She pointed at her one-eyed husband. "He didn't have any fancy architectural training." She flung her arms wide to indicate the impressive living room. "That's the kind of man he was. And now you have his eyeball on a pin..." She downed her wine and poured another glass.

"Your anger is healthy," the young doctor said. He set the eyeball on the coffee table and joined her on the couch. Gently, he folded the corners of her napkin over the vase shards. "Do this later, darling. Even God rested once a week."

She understood that he was talking about more than the vase. She had taken to repairing every object her husband had broken since his illness. For three months, reparations had been her top priority, at times neglecting to feed herself or her husband.

They heard the side door open and close. Sneakers squeaked through the kitchen and up the stairs.

"She's not adjusting," the wife said. "I signed over the Cherokee. She *owns* it. I bought her a new wardrobe – does she even care? I never thought I'd say it, but I wish my mom and dad were still around. She could live with them and see what the alternative is."

"Look at this," the young doctor said. He reached down, retrieved the pin, and brought the eyeball close to the wife's face.

She studied it. "The color isn't right."

"See how dark and flimsy these are?" He flicked the dangling fibers. "A healthy eyeball doesn't tear so easily. The lens, the receptors...shriveled like prunes. That eyebrow laceration should have bled rivers. Come with me."

Taking her hand, he pulled her down to the carpet, beside the husband.

"Compare the skin of the arm to the skin of the face."

"Yes," the wife said. The face was gray. She wondered if she had noticed but hadn't been able to acknowledge it.

"Soon, the head will be black. Then, the stench."

He showed her other things. The husband's sinuses and mouth had stopped producing moisture. His nostrils were inflamed and red. His tongue had swelled to twice its size. With a gentle tug, a clump of hair detached from the husband's scalp.

"Try the teeth," the young doctor said.

The wife reached past the cracked lips, into her husband's mouth. She plucked out an incisor. One by one, she yanked his remaining teeth and formed a tidy pile on the carpet. Then she cradled his head and removed his hair, which felt like pulling weeds. With a few brushes of her fingertips, his eyebrows scattered like pollen.

The husband didn't struggle. His breathing was slow and deep. Inside him, the darkness was saturated with light. He could see. He floated on a river under a pale sky. He felt clean and untroubled, and when he tried to recall his life before this moment, he saw only blue, and he understood that the blue was him.

The young doctor had gone to his car, and now he returned with a surgical saw and black medical bag. "Does your daughter want to watch?"

"If she does, she wouldn't admit it."

The young doctor nodded. "But a word to the wise – she might never forgive you for doing this without her."

The wife gathered her husband's teeth. She unfolded the cloth napkin and mixed the teeth with the vase shards. Then she carried the bundle to the kitchen.

"Grab the cutting board while you're in there!" the doctor called.

The kitchen lights were off, but she could see by the moon. She tossed the napkin into the garbage below the sink. She brought a fresh bottle from the pantry, uncorked it, and poured a glass. From upstairs, the daughter's music resounded: *Sometimes when the cuckoo's crying, when the moon is halfway down / Sometimes when the night is dying, I take me out and I wander around.*

In the living room, the young doctor had rolled the husband onto his stomach. Couch cushions elevated his torso. Obeying the young doctor's gesture, the wife slid the cutting board under the husband's face.

The young doctor wriggled his fingers into latex gloves. "Force of habit," he admitted, somberly.

The wife's hands shook so badly she had to set her wine on the coffee table. She'd thought she was prepared, but her face felt numb. She tapped a cigarette out of the pack. She noticed that the young doctor was staring at her with his insistent, demanding eyes.

"I don't want to bilk you out of your money. I love you. And I make more than you, anyway."

The wife wasn't sure she'd heard correctly.

The teenage daughter appeared in the entryway in her pajamas. Black eyeliner, dripping, had clowned her cheeks. Her hands bore a stack of paper.

"Is that a report for school?" the wife asked. "Not now, darling."

The daughter scoffed. "It's a report for life, Mom." She stepped into the living room and regarded the husband, who lay face down and hogtied upon the couch cushions. "Kind of ironic," she smirked. Her lips trembled.

"No," the young doctor corrected. "It's a surgical procedure."

The daughter padded across the carpet, barefoot, aggressive. "It's *ironic*," she hissed. She tossed the papers at the young doctor's face, but he deflected them with a raised forearm.

"What was that music in your room?" the wife said.

"What are you doing to my daddy?"

"It's simple," the young doctor started.

"I didn't ask you!" the daughter shouted. "This is his book." She indicated the scattered sheets. "If you had bothered to read it, you would know that grandpa was beheaded in Vietnam. Or maybe you did read it. Maybe that's where you got the idea! Copying a war crime – I wouldn't put it past you!"

"I assure you," the young doctor said, displaying no discernible emotion, "that this is a necessary precaution to save your father's life."

With these words, the daughter wilted. The young doctor embraced her, patting her back. She cried into his shoulder. "Please do the honors," he whispered.

He reached into his bag. He put the saw into the daughter's hands and then found a seat near the wife's legs, one of which he stroked reassuringly.

The daughter, on hands and knees, crawled to the husband's head. She lowered the blade and seemed to watch from a great distance as the teeth bit into the papery skin. For a full minute, she sawed. At last, the head separated from the body. The young doctor said, "Well done," and snipped the remaining veins with scissors.

Nothing changed. The husband's body lay in repose. A few drops of blood stained the cutting board. The young doctor presented the hairless head to the wife's lap. The single eye stared. The gummy mouth hung open.

The daughter sawed the ropes that bound the husband's wrists. Then she stood. She embraced the young doctor. She kissed his hair and said, "You smell nice."

The husband's headless body rolled onto its back. It sat upright and bear-hugged the young doctor's waist. The young doctor made a low noise of despair in his throat when he realized he couldn't break free.

The husband pinned him to the floor. The wife, whose tears fell on the husband's face, heard the young doctor grunt, "Please don't," when the teenage daughter came at him.

The wife saw her daughter crouching beside the young doctor, and she understood what was happening. Her chest vibrated with pride. *Of course*, she thought.

The wife was surprised that the young doctor continued to speak while the saw teeth cut into his neck. His panicked eyes found the wife. He said, "Stop this. Touch him." The blade sunk deeper. Blood rose and spilled. He said, weakly, "You love me," and then his words were gargles. His spinal cord severed with a dull pop. In death, his eyes defaulted to desperation.

Two headless men spooned in the blooming pool.

Panting, the daughter held aloft the young doctor's head. "It's heavier than I thought," she remarked.

But the mother was not within earshot. She was running up the stairs, running with purpose to the bedroom in search of the sewing kit.

Ha-Ha, Shirt

Shirt has something sweet he isn't giving up, but it's tucked into a front pocket of his jeans and so is impossible to get at from my position on the dance floor, where I'm busy doing a solo gyration and blinking to create a strobe effect. I keep reaching out to grab at it, but what the fuck am I doing because I'm ten feet away from him and that sweet thing in his pocket keeps bumping against the upper thigh of Mizz Offset Breasts, who has a fine pair of legs but seems to have lost the battle of the brush this morning, judging by the chicken-wing protruding off the back of her head. And those tits are not appealing in any way, although every last one of my buddies'll tell you I'm your man when it comes to tits. Big-nippled, one-nippled, risen or deflated, mouthful or three-course, sweaty-bottomed or rashed, I've appreciated them all. Never had crooked ones, though, and maybe because of my missing contact lens, looking at them is making me nauseous and I need to sit down.

Shirt must like what he sees in Lopsided because him and Double-Decker are groping and grappling and getting all twisted together, making out with tongues and licking whatever they can get away with licking in public. I come barside and lean over to Ha-Ha and say I might puke if he buys me a scotch and so he does, but he spits in it to make me earn it.

It isn't an aggressive gesture coming from Ha-Ha, though from anyone else it certainly would be. But no, I gotta include

Shirt because he's as good a friend as Ha-Ha. I mostly feel close to Ha-Ha, and swapping fluids like blood brothers is a natural way to show our connectedness. We ended up at the Club Go-Go without reason or desire only because Shirt declared his physical illness at being in close quarters with me and Ha-Ha during our regular weekly cruise around Kalamazoo. He said "Fuck you both, your breath stinks," and now Ha-Ha screams in my ear what sounds like a song, "You and me are on the same page, my friend, same page." He *tink-tinks* my glass with his and down go the shots, mine burning enough inside to make me holler, "God fuck the little children! I got a paycheck!"

Me and Ha-Ha, through loud shouting conversation, decide that enough is enough, friends like us should inform their buddy when he's making an error. Shirt has been less than himself lately, and only by being with his chums, and not this skin-and-bones woman, can he truly be the Shirt we've come to love.

"Because there ain't shoes in his shoebox," Ha-Ha's tilted, puddly mouth is HEY-HEYing in my left ear. "Son of a bitch in tears on his bed and he won't talk to me and he's got a shoebox on his lap and you ain't telling me there's SHOES in that box? No way!"

Pretty soon we drag Shirt's ass outta there because I have a sudden puke problem all across the bar, which makes the bouncer vise my shoulder and escort me outside. He won't let me touch his hand, the gripping one, even though I rub my face on it and say, "I'm such a pretty pretty kitten." Fucknut pulls my hair to make me stop and calls me a homo fuck as his exit from the scene.

Shirt and Ha-Ha come outside and find me sitting on the pavement, and it isn't yet 2:00 A.M. so we drive to the Hot-N-Now for olive burgers to fill our stomachs, which is good except Shirt makes a scene in the drive-thru and winds up crushing an olive burger in his fist and shaking it at the lady and yelling "This is extremely cheap!" with a lot of conviction and intensity while the burger guts fall all over him and the silver ledge of the burger window. I try to salvage some of the massacre from his lap after we pay less than what we owe and gun it, but Shirt knocks my hand away and tells me to eat my own goddamn burger, which I do.

Shirt's fast-food mutilation and drive-thru harassment are funny-but-loud reminders of the recent change in his disposition. For two years I've called Shirt a friend and for those same two years he's been grieving the suicide of his father, which to hear him tell it was a surprise but not surprising, and every time he distinctions this way I understand a little bit more what he means, like hearing the same New Testament readings over and over in church, but as your life changes, so do the words, even though you've heard them a thousand times before and even can remember them from when you were a child.

Shirt's grieving has never been violent. Most always he's quiet and tucked into himself, which I generally perceive to be a sign of wisdom. He's a carpenter by trade, skilled at putting up walls and whatnot, but business according to Ha-Ha suffers lately from Shirt's oversleeping and his verbal outbursts against his brother Phil, who just last week finally said Screw It All and moved to Louisiana to run a telemarketing office. This, and the shoebox speculation, and the three-weeks-ago home removal of his own dead molar with a pair of pliers, and now the olive burger massacre, are all alterations to the Shirt I know, but how can I fucking see when I've got only one contact lens and can't stop winking back and forth between blur clear blur clear blur clear?

It isn't until we get back to Ha-Ha/Shirt's and I try unsuccessfully to get either of them to fuck me or let me fuck them, that I remember Shirt has something sweet in his pocket, only now I can't remember what it is, and can't think of it because Ha-Ha's calling me a faggot with a cigarette dangling from his mouth while he works the Nintendo controller. This macho talk is typical of Ha-Ha only when we're with Shirt, which lately is always. Shirt has a power thing over his roommate that makes Ha-Ha behave against his natural inclinations, which are to be nonjudgmental and to fuck me or let me fuck him, if and when the fancy strikes. Shirt's power thing doesn't work on me, so there's a triangle with the three of us – me and Ha-Ha secure enough to once in a while release our sexual buildups when women aren't convenient, Shirt mouthless and intent on ignoring but never unkind. At the moment I can visualize the triangle above my face as a glowing shape rotating in the air.

So I'm singing at the top of my lungs one of the worst songs ever written, which is Leavin on a Jet Plane by that fuck John fuck whatever. I'll suck a dick. I don't care about it. We all got needs and I'll suck the dick of a friend if it helps get that shit out of your system. No different than helping a buddy jack-up his car and replace the exhaust. I ain't a faggot by any stretch. I just like to fuck people when I'm drunk because it feels nice to have an orgasm with company and women are a bitch to get rid of sometimes. Ha-Ha backs me up on this! Even though he won't look at me right now and his ashes are dropping all over his Nintendo controller. Most guys think I'm queer for saying it, but you know what? They just aren't honest.

We sit around and farewell a twelve-pack, then I'm handed the whiskey bottle, the regular Saturday night routine playing out like clockwork. I'm thinking about how this is no less valid than the church routine I'll be practicing in about seven hours, us here with the same type of devotion only no prayers except internal ones directed at no God in particular and not prescribed to us by the Good Book. We're each doing our own thing, Ha-Ha at the video game pushing buttons and smoke-blowing, Shirt throwing karate kicks, knocking down a lamp, me speaking in tongues on my back while my mind makes pictures of Sarah and me and our baby daughter on the bandage-looking ceiling.

The unbelievable well of Sarah's insides and the buckets of it she wastes on me! It makes me want to puke again so I go face-down into the carpet but nothing comes out, so I lick lick lick the carpet and think about forming a hairball in my gut and pray the hairball on the way back up will taste like Jim Beam. For six years now she's borne my sexual misdeeds with women I'd barely met and sometimes men and of course the magnificent squeaky plastic LuLu. And even though Sarah only knows about a single digit portion of these intercourses, just the fact that she keeps forgiving and forgiving is a knife in my brain, because I know it damages her. She isn't any pushover, but she has a heart and knows how to live, I suppose, in a true Christian fashion, whereas I've been only gestures and words for a long while now and sometimes can't remember how Sarah dressed when she taught at the elementary school, or what the third-graders gave her as presents because now they're in a dusty box in the basement because I insisted that Sarah didn't need to work anymore, that the baby was the most important thing, and that I, the man, would make our ends meet. I can still hear that goddamn hi-lo beeping and that motherfucker Don – bless him because he tried – yelling in his cough-drop voice from across the warehouse, "Look out!" I didn't look out. I never look out.

I'm practically puking, slamming my never-hurt foot on the floor, and there's a tremendous knock at the door, like a cop knock. I sit up ready to pound some cop ass.

Turns out it's the cab driver they called to get me the fuck out of their apartment. I'm pissed at Shirt and tell him so, and he points at me and says, "Get home. Get outta here." He pushes me through the door. I don't notice much about the cab ride except putting out my cigarette on the back of the driver's seat and getting yelled at. On my front lawn I fall down, which bruises my forearm on a tree root, but I make it inside to Sarah and my daughter in one piece.

Sarah's asleep on the couch with the television glowing blue, some neglected connection. I go upstairs to remove my contact lens and put on my glasses. I grab a porno from my dresser and bring it downstairs, pop it in the DVD, and kneel in front of the screen so if she wakes she won't be able to readily identify the screen action. Over the years I've perfected my masturbation techniques, which you would think would make the sexual act unnecessary but actually just feeds the fire. I shoot a wad onto the carpet, rub it clean with a paper towel, catch my breath, go to the kitchen for another beer.

I repeat this ritual an hour later after a bedside with the baby where I sipped and stared and wondered what the hell this child would turn out like, hoping she would not eventually hate her father. I hear the birds chirping outside as I'm wiping off my hand and figure I'd best get off to bed because that's what people do. I leave Sarah on the couch.

I can't sleep, thinking about how long I can get away with drawing workman's comp. Half a year ago, hobbled by breaks in metatarsals, proximals, distals in the toes, now the foot is month-long fine. Still, I grimace and "Ouch!" for the doctor. Muscle damage is tougher to disprove. Checks keep coming, also phone calls every two days from Don the foreman, asking "How's it coming?" I can wiggle my toes, do a jig, but I say, "I'm in a lot of pain, Don. Doctor says maybe another month." Sarah turns both cheeks, acts like she doesn't hear. I keep thinking that maybe out in the bushes eventually will be a FraudBusters with a video camera who'll pass the tape to a judge, who'll send me to Jackson, and I'll lose my wife and baby.

About six o'clock the phone rings, and I pick it up before the first ring dies. It's Shirt, saying that Ha-Ha's sleeping, and "I want to smoke some weed and show you what's in my pocket." I search his voice for signs of anger, but he's sloshed. That's my assessment. He's got something in his pocket and he thinks I want to see it, and maybe I do but I can't remember what it is. Either way, smoking a little grass sounds all right.

I re-dress while a headache makes itself known above my eyebrows. I kiss the baby with lips stuck out so as not to stubble her, and remember the time Sarah caught me in the bedroom fucking LuLu the blow-up doll. It looked funny, me going at it with a piece of plastic, but after we got married, Sarah wouldn't admit anything humorous in it at all and made me sign up for free counseling at the Y, although later I could make her chuckle about it if she had a glass of bourbon in her and I'd been good for a while.

Just as I'm finishing my cigarette, Shirt drives up in his Buick Skylark with the one mini-spare on the left rear. I climb in. I don't like the way he's kneading the wheel like a breadstick. He appears crazy. His right eyelid is low and lazy, reminding me of my dad, who looked the same when he was drunk and soaking in the bathtub with a bag of Doritos in his hands.

Shirt's very nearly the highest I've seen him in the two years since our acquaintance-making at the Déjà Vu, which is a lot of days and a lot of highs ago. He's honking at trees, screaming *Let the niggers free! They'll help us manage the banks!* running up the curbs when we turn corners, goosing the engine, giving the windshield five, six, seven, eight – fucking hell, man, stop it already! – hose downs with fluid without wiping it off. It's a mess, and I ream him for smoking without me, seeing that I have to be back home in three hours in order to make ten o'clock mass with the family. Shirt hates to think about God or the House of God, or all the prayers floating up into the sky without his name attached to them. He turns to me and says, in a slowed-down voice, that I, especially, should understand, because God's a vibrator and going to church is like sitting on a vibrator. I take his meaning to be that church-going is pleasurable but phony and without any lasting emotional value. I mostly agree with him. However, I can see the need in our lives for pleasurable-but-phony activities, but I don't say as much, figuring now's not the time to argue.

Shirt pulls to the curb in front of a 7-11. He turns off the engine and hollers at me for not letting him get with Lopsided Double-Decker Tits, only he refers to her as "Anna" so it takes me a few minutes to understand. He says he hasn't gotten any in about forty weeks. A genuine sadness sets up shop on his face. He's on the tubby side, doesn't shave often enough, has pockmarks on his cheeks, probably from the High School Acne Wars, and looks out at the world through minuscule, beady eyes. It's easy to see the reason for his drought.

I tell him straight up that if it's fucking he wants then we should just go on and do it. It makes me cranky thinking we drove around for twenty minutes doing everything but flashing a neon sign saying "DUI" when all he's looking for is an orgasm that could be attained without the delay that's gonna cause me another sleep-free evening on the planet Earth.

Nothing of the nice Shirt appears in his eyes when he looks at me. It's a bitter look, watery and unforgiving. He says to stop it with that shit, to stop it once and for all. I say I wasn't making a command but only a suggestion. I try to explain again about biology, and our great human ability to interact with the world inside our imaginations. I tell him that wasting this gift is like a slap in the face to God himself. He puts his hard hand over my mouth and tells me that Ha-Ha is taking my bullshit seriously. He says that this very evening, after I left, Ha-Ha climbed into bed and tried to fuck him against his will. Shirt's crying at this point, his fingers clamping tighter on my cheekbones. He says Ha-Ha got a beating because of me and that I need to just quit.

I push his hand off. My mind says one thing loudly: "Ha-Ha would not force anybody to do anything, least of all to please him sexually." If this is not true, then the formula I've used to evaluate my friends is not the proper formula. In my mind Shirt is the dominant one in their household, the quiet, shoebox-hiding, self-dentalizing, lamp-kicking one, the one who needs to look at himself for a good long while before passing judgment. I tell him this, then hop out of the car and run up to the 7-11. I figure I can't buy a beer, but I can steal one.

When I come out, Shirt's gone. I look up and down the surrounding streets for any sign of the Buick, but I get nothing. I can't dally for long because of the frigid forty-ouncer under my shirt. I head home.

The sun is just coming up to light my way. This makes me happy. So too does the golden quality of the sunlight, the sharpness of the air being sucked into my nose. I feel sober again. Sober, tired, and thirsty. I see a rabbit hopping in the junkyard across the street and wonder if it's actually the owner under the spell of some demon witch hag. I know that demon witch hags still exist in this world, having fucked two of them last month. I see a Herby-Curby tipped over with its guts spilled out onto the road. The flies are feasting. A woman passes me driving a Chevy S10 pickup. She makes me feel bad about something with the way her eyes flash at me. It has to be a lie, what Shirt said about Ha-Ha. If it isn't, then Ha-Ha is no one's friend. The yeasty King Cobra stench under my nose is better than the taste going down. I have a headache. Ha-Ha is my friend, although it was Shirt who introduced me to him. Does that make Shirt the superior officer? Ha-Ha – what now, five or six months? – I suppose is not allowed onto the level of long-term where I place Shirt and Sarah, and even the baby pulls rank at ten months. Ha-Ha has held three different jobs in this past half-year...is that a sign of evil? Me with no job, I'm not to say. I pull long from my King Cobra, my goal being to finish the bottle before arriving home.

I put the empty bottle in a sack in the kitchen. Sarah's upstairs running the faucet, making her preparations. The baby's crying, which always gets a response from me, so I climb the staircase, take her from the crib and hold her and sway.

We make it to church on time. Sarah sticks her cold shoulder in my face the whole morning, but when we we're kneeling I use my hands to make shadow puppets on the pew in front of us, which makes her smile. The baby's a sweetheart, not sleeping but looking at all the praying with big eyes, trying to absorb everything. When the time is upon us we join the communion line. The music is solemn and the people are orderly to the point of creepiness, moving stone-faced, almost sad, up the aisles. I take the body of Christ into my mouth, sip more than what's appropriate at the cup of blood, go back to the pew to kneel and munch the wafer. This is where I'm supposed to ponder my life circumstances, which is always difficult for me, being forced to drop my natural thoughts and replace them with as much unnatural reflection and conciliation as will fit into three minutes. I send God a brain telegraph suggesting He protect the little ones like my daughter and make every storm have a rainbow at the end of it. I laugh out loud at this, bringing an elbow jab from the wife.

On the drive home, I don't think about anything but my head kissing the pillow, but when we get there and open the door, it shocks me like a radio in the bathtub to see Shirt in our living room, pointing a pistol at our faces. He's dark under the eyes and bloodshot in his whites, and next to my recliner, which he's sitting in, is his goddamn shoebox, open and empty and on its side like a wrecked car.

He tells us to stop right there and to do whatever he says. His hair's sculpted into a cone, though I doubt he knows about his hair shape. Sweat's beaded on his forehead. Sarah's "You've got to be kidding me!" gives the baby a reason to scream so before I know it the scene's chaotic. I tell Shirt to let me put the baby away because I don't like guns to be in the same room with her, and Shirt obliges, maybe out of kindness but maybe out of the desire to not kill a baby. I take her upstairs and set her in the crib and coo-coo for a minute while I dial 911, but I don't feel comfortable knowing there's a gun being brandished at my wife, so I head back downstairs, just after I whisper the details to the emergency lady and hang up.

After a lot of bullshit despondency and gesticulating and tears from Shirt, it finally comes out that he wants to fuck Sarah. I get pissed off at that. Sarah's naturally terrified and disbelieving. She lets loose like she has let loose on me before, only this time without a whiff of affection, telling Shirt to shut up and get out of our lives and back to his house and to leave us alone, once and for all. The baby's a miniature echo from upstairs, only she's not making real words.

I cut in and say, "No, Shirt. You can't touch her." Nothing in my book is more evil and wrong than forcing sex on a person, and there's no way Sarah's having it, even to avoid being shot, so I call Shirt a few more names and say if he wants to do someone just to do me and move on with life so none of us has to die or be put into a compromising position.

He knows he's wrong. I can see in his eyes the lack of conviction, the confusion. I've only been good toward him and he knows it, and I can see this thought bouncing around in his brain. He takes off his shirt, which reminds us of why he's called Shirt. His fear of skin cancer means he never disrobes while outside on the job, and as a result he's constantly bearing a deep tan on his arms and neck, leaving his torso as pale as the underside of a rock after a rain. It's a nickname that Ha-Ha gave him, even though he never asked for it.

He wants to be in command, telling me to bend over and pull down my pants. I follow his suggestion.

I hear him undoing his trousers. I'm pretty sure it's a tear that drips onto my backside as he pushes up my shirt. He keeps muttering under his breath, things like *Fuckin fag, I'm gonna fuck you, you little shit, you faggot cunt,* while I focus my stare on the wood grain of the end table upon which I'm resting my chin. My ears are focused on Sarah's mouth-covered crying, and I realize that for a long time I've been hoping for a way to tell her, 'I'm a terrible man,' and *mean* it, mean it that her repeated love and forgiveness, while intensely kind, is only deepening my grief in ways indescribable. I think in this moment that my bending over with naked asshole parted, naked asshole ready and able to take the rape meant for her, is the only way I can tell her that I'm truly terrible, truly terrible and terribly sorry, and to please please stop forgiving me, *please,* because I will never stop hurting you.

"Go on, you desperate prick," I yell at Shirt. "Get going, we ain't got all day!"

It probably isn't a good idea to provoke him, but I can't help myself, being scared as I am, and my daughter upstairs like a shrieking teapot, and my wife watching a re-enactment of what she has probably already had nightmares about. The motherfucker has a gun pointed at her. And there's that empty shoebox, just like Ha-Ha said, not three feet from my left arm. And it's as useless as Shirt's dick.

He's half-hard, poking at me. Sarah's bawling, and I tell her to *shhh* because everything is gonna be fine once Limp Dick finishes satisfying himself, which makes Shirt step back and kick me a couple times in the ribs. It's an ugly moment; I've never known Shirt to do anything violent to anything other than a lamp and recently his molar, and I truly have believed all along that we are friends. Here he is about to rape me after wanting to rape my wife and on top of it all bruising my ribs and giving me breathing difficulties. I reevaluate things in the slowed-down seconds, my friendships, my behavior, the way sex talks to a man louder than any other voice he can hear. I've never been the poster child for celibacy, having fucked inflatables and twelve women and five men during the course of my four-year marriage, but in my heart I cannot believe that what I've done is cruel and this here is dirty and cruel and evil.

We all hear the sirens while he rams fruitlessly against me. I'm surprised he doesn't blow my head apart the instant they come into earshot, but I suspect he has no ill will toward me, and is rather experiencing a destructive impulse toward his own life. Although I did phone the police while upstairs with my daughter, I will not admit this no matter how loudly Shirt curses me to do so.

There's a pause, during which Shirt's breathing is the predominant sound – I can sense him back there, can't see him because my eyes are closed; he's a vibration behind me and above me – and I can smell my Jesus-blood breath in my cupped hand. Then I hear the gunshot. It's nothing more than a tiny *pop!* and for a split second I feel disappointed by it.

I'm left relatively dry until his body falls on top of me. Then there's blood everywhere, most of it hot and gushing out of his face all over my back. I'm unable to move under the sloppy commotion. His body twitches on me for about five seconds, making movements like he's really trying to fuck me, with his cock finally feeling hard and everything, until Sarah kicks him off. She comes up on me and tells me everything's okay. The cops storm inside and confirm that Shirt is dead and that Sarah and I aren't injured and that there's a bullet lodged in the corner of the ceiling above the television.

They find a condom in his pocket, Trojan brand. It surprises me, while I'm being toweled by Sarah and pen-lighted by the paramedics, that this rubber was the item I was so fixated upon during the previous night's festivities. I keep this detail a secret from Sarah because it seems like the thing to do.

•••

They bury Shirt in the cemetery near his mother's house three days later. Sarah couldn't bring herself to clean up the blood and goo on the floor and ceiling, and I can't say I blamed her. You'd have thought the cops would take care of it, but they did a half-assed job as they enjoy doing with most things. The floor cleaned up no problem. I scrubbed the wall area for thirty minutes, then gave up because the pink hue wouldn't go away. I brought a half-gallon of white paint up from the basement and gave the spot a new coat.

I'm tipsy at the funeral home, but nothing compared to the way I've been for the weeks and months preceding. My foot has been healed up for about thirty days and I've been milking my workman's comp – this fact is a city bus in my mind, passing by hour after hour, day after day – and I experience a little revelation when I see the corpse of Randall Paris Jerome in his coffin and hear his cousins, aunts and uncles, mother, and even his brother Phil from Louisiana, crying into their handkerchiefs. I decide right then that unless something major comes up, I'll definitely go back to the moving company within a week or two, as a way of reacquainting myself with humanity.

Out in the graveyard, they're still making a lot of noise while the priest tries to outshout them and the wind. All I catch from Father Vincent is, "I gave my heart to know wisdom, and to know madness and folly," and then, a few minutes later, "Amen."

To these people, what Shirt did or didn't do doesn't matter. There is a stock of tears set aside for him that they'll use. Even after his *psychotic break*, which is the term heard thirty times around the funeral home, even after having his dick and his pistol poke me in invasive ways – even after all this, even I spit out a few tears.

I'm busy concentrating on the shiny casket, avoiding eye contact with Ha-Ha. His face is there, across the pit, between Louisiana Phil and Louisiana Phil's wife. One of Ha-Ha's eyes has clearly been whacked by something solid. People are laying hands on the casket for the last time, saying their good-byes, walking away. I don't feel like touching anything. I stand rooted, and chew my gum with my mouth closed.

After the coffin sinks into the ground, Ha-Ha walks up and hugs me. His right eye is puffed shut and the color of a mulberry. It feels wrong now, hugging Ha-Ha, what with Shirt's accusation. The swollen eye is like Shirt's beyond-the-grave message – *see, I told you!*

I don't want to know the truth. At this point it's all words, anyway. We walk up the hill toward the parking lot. To make him think that I think that none of this was his fault, I tell Ha-Ha that Shirt was bottled up and sexually frustrated, and that near as I could figure this was the reason for his insanity. Ha-Ha says he suspected as much, with the way Shirt had acted for a long time now. He discloses to me that Shirt used to come into his room and jack off when he thought Ha-Ha was asleep.

Ha-Ha sips from a flask and shares a few belts with me. It tastes like Jim Beam, only cheaper. He says that Shirt was never violent toward him, that this *shiner* is from Shirt accidentally elbowing him in the face when they were playing Nintendo after I left the other night. Every word he says comes out all covered in shit. We smoke and he talks. It troubles me that the message his eyes flash is not what's going on inside his head. I want to confront him with Shirt's version of the shiner, but I don't. I yawn.

Once the cigarettes are squashed under our shoes, we shake hands. I watch Ha-Ha climb into his truck, knowing he'll never call me again and that I won't call him either, and that if we see one another across the pool tables at the Green Top, we'll pretend we're seeing strangers. This certain alliance is finished.

Mouth

There's a mouth in my closet, the boy said.

Don't be silly. You mean monster.

Yes.

No, kiddo. There's never a monster.

It's a certain kind of monster.

The mother laughed. I've known monsters like that.

The lamp clicked. Black detour.

It's grainy, the boy said. It fills up the whole closet. He thought: *Don't leave. Don't do anything where I can't smell your dress.*

Grainy. I think you're asleep, kiddo.

I meant bumpy. It told me to climb on its tongue.

And let me guess. You did.

Yes.

She covered him.

You're shivering.

I'm not cold.

Would you like me to open the closet and show you?

The boy didn't answer.

I'll get another blanket. She slapped her arms. Your father needs to look at that heater.

The mouth never closes, the boy whispered.

Sounds like a dependable mouth, the mother said.

Her face defied the darkness, a lacework of treed moonlight upon her skin.

She arrived at the closet. She turned the handle.

To the boy, the mouth had called itself Miss Begotten, Miss Shapen.

But it was not a woman, exactly. Full of teeth large as heads.

Barney Hester

So what about this girl? The one who hyperextended that inhuman jawbone to vacuum up my best friend? It took me fifteen years of therapy and ten years (running) of prescription drugs to convince me that it isn't normal behavior for girls to swallow the boys who like them. Even after all that, I continue to see her cavernous maw in every footprint in the snow, every dark hole in the trunk of a tree. Whenever a baby screams for its bottle, I hear Barney.

Women in general still terrify me. For fifteen years, the act of sex was ruined: Her mouth was in a different place, the head wasn't at the top of my body, but the gesture was the same.

Her name was Tanya. This is a false name. I swore to her that I would never reveal her identity. (Although I suppose the Hesters, should they ever read this, would be able to supply it. No matter.) I will never break my promise. I urinated in my pants as I made that vow. Urinating in one's pants is funny, in theory and in movies. When it actually happens, when the body and mind shut down, when you feel that you are imploding upon yourself – then it's nothing to laugh about. The simple act of documenting this experience is enough to set in motion those soundless fears, those fears that she will appear at my doorstep or my window, tapping to be let in. I can see her smiling out there. Her eyes are black. Her teeth are white.

•••

Behind the Hesters' house stood an expanse of wooded land, maybe ten acres. More undeveloped acreage – wooded, barren, grassy – on every side of their house gave the area a lonely, forgotten feel. The birds and crickets were louder than the cars. Barney used to tell me that the woman down the street, their nearest neighbor at two hundred yards away, mowed her lawn topless. This just proves how isolated these people were, on the outskirts of Grand Rapids, close to the Rockford border.

•••

One time at the Hesters', I stayed later than I'd intended. It was autumn; the sun abandoned us early. Nightfall descended swiftly and painlessly. Barney and I lay on our bellies in the basement, engrossed in our hand-held Coleco electronic football game. Ozzy Osbourne sang *Fairies Wear Boots* from Danny's room next door.

When 8:00 P.M. rolled around I told Barney I had to go home, so he waited until I wasn't ready, reared back, and leveled me with a punch to the gut. I folded. Then he ran upstairs and told his mom that I'd spit on the carpet. I walked out of the house trying to hold back the tears. My stomach clenched and I was having difficulty breathing. I hopped on my Huffy and rode away.

Normally I made a point of riding as quickly as possible until I reached the Beltline, which was the main road. On that night I could barely pedal. Sitting upright was an enormous job. It was a long, dark, sloping street. Small mammals scurried into the shadows along the shoulder. I'm not sure if the surroundings frightened Barney, his older brother Danny, or his younger sister Margaret. They never seemed scared of anything.

That bike ride physically altered me forever. For reasons I've never been certain of, I lost my balance and fell over the handlebars, directly onto my face. That's why to this day I have a crooked nose and a crimped upper lip. My front teeth were loose, my mouth was filled with blood. I raised my head, spitting. I had fallen in front of somebody's house; as I looked up, a light in the living room extinguished. Reflecting now, for what it's worth, I know it was Tanya's house.

•••

Here are some facts:
1) Barney Hester, at the age of twelve, was swallowed by this girl, whom he loved.
2) I didn't try to stop her.
3) Barney didn't struggle as his head disappeared into her mouth. His arms remained flat at his sides. He did, however, scream like an unfed infant.
4) I loved Barney Hester.
5) He tried to kill me.

•••

After the punching incident and the ensuing bicycle mishap (which I also blamed on him) I vowed never to talk to Barney again. As usual, I was weak. He lured me back with his seductive charm, and promises of abandoned *Penthouses* hidden in the weeds behind his house. He was a handsome boy. Even then, in fifth grade, I knew this, and I realize now this was part of his hold on me. He had the confidence and swagger that good-looking males inevitably adopt. The fifth-grade girls used whatever means necessary to steal his personal effects – a cutout football he made for a school project, a broken shoelace, his trademark black combs (he had a bucketful in his room) – and sneak to the corner of the classroom to cover them with kisses. The other boys used to get pissed off at this behavior. Not from jealousy, mind you, but because they thought it was insulting to our gender. Barney didn't mind the attention. He smirked about it.

His big brother used to wallop the living crap out of him. Maybe that's why I cut Barney so much slack. Gangly, red-haired Danny's evening ritual was to sit on Barney's chest and play the drums on his face. With drumsticks. He whipped Barney's naked butt with wet towels until the skin broke open. He gave Barney Indian burns for not doing his chores. He tied Barney up inside the abandoned doghouse for *doing* his chores. He made Barney eat moldy cheese for not doing *Danny's* chores. His parents turned a blind eye to this terrorism partly because his mother was blind, literally (since birth), and partly because his father weighed 500 pounds. Mr. Hester seemed almost too fat to move; chasing down and punishing Danny even once would've equaled more exercise than Mr. Hester got in a month. Theirs was a grotesque family. Even his little sister, with her innocent-looking plaid Catholic-school skirt, was not exempt from bearing their unsavory genes; she is an albino.

I'll lay off Margaret now. She's the one who cooks my meals and sleeps beside me at night. I won't risk losing those things. We're married. And she has nothing to do with the Hesters – her own family – anymore. I love her. When I'm in her, I'm not afraid. I don't worry about never coming out again.

●●●

After Barney Hester disappeared, some people claimed that he'd been a genius. Not true. People always try to glorify the victim. He cheated on tests in school. I saw him do it. As a matter of fact, I was often "coerced" (read: bullied) by Barney into supplying him with answers. His spelling was primitive. His implementation of the scientific method consisted of seeing how many BBs a garter snake could be shot with before it finally croaked. If it somehow turns out that Barney faked his disappearance, his own swallowing, at the age of twelve, then maybe I would concede that he is a genius. An acting genius for sure.

Sometimes, even after all these years, I look for him. I still live in Grand Rapids. It's a big enough city. It would have been easy for him to be absorbed into the streets. He could've become a prostitute, a thief, a gambler, a gambling prostitute thief. Any of those romantic things.

When his parents discovered that Barney was gone, they spent a good deal of their money searching for him. I still have the milk carton with his face and statistics on it:

Barney James Hester
Five feet tall
Age 12
Born November 12, 1970
Red hair
One dimple in his cheek when he smiles
Weighs 94 pounds
Last seen wearing a blue Detroit Lions jersey with number 17 and the word "Hipple" on the back.

For as much as his folks professed to care about him after he was devoured, it's worth mentioning that I had to provide the police with all the above information, except for age and hair color. My story for the cops, by the way, was that Barney had simply run into the woods for no apparent reason. That was the last I saw of him.

●●●

My first clue that Barney had fallen in love was the smell of Dove soap. One day, his hands reeked of it. He'd never smelled like anything other than burped-up Cheetos and bologna sandwiches, so the change was pretty obvious. I found out later that he was washing himself in excess of ten times a day. If he wasn't showering or taking a bath, he was scrubbing – face, neck, arms, hands – any area he could reach in his two-minute trips to the bathroom. One day his book bag spilled and four bars of Dove tumbled onto the floor. I wanted to mock him for his new hygienic obsession, but I couldn't. He looked so damn pathetic kneeling down to pick them up. I also didn't want to get punched.

Talking to Barney wasn't something one could just "do." The moment had to be right, and it had to be on Barney's terms. Most days he showed no emotion other than anger and apathy. If he laughed, it was at somebody else's misfortune. He talked tough. He talked football, MTV, cigarettes, bikes, boobs. I don't think he ever talked about food. Food didn't interest him unless it was covered with cheese.

Once in a while, however, Barney opened up. It was impossible to predict when this would happen. After baseball practice one day, we walked to my house. On the shoulder of the road we came across a dead squirrel. It was crushed and split open, with flies dancing on it. Expecting Barney to lift it by the tail and hurl it at me, I started running. Eventually, I turned around. He hadn't moved. He was staring down at the squirrel. I went back.

He said, "I don't think this was an accident."

"You think somebody killed it?"

"Of course somebody killed it. But they didn't mean to."

"You should go look up the word 'accident.'"

"This squirrel committed suicide."

Then he told me about his Uncle Lincoln, who had shot himself with an old Army pistol. He said it wasn't really a tragedy since his uncle had wanted to die. Even his family agreed. Everyone was sad and everything, because Linc had been a good guy, but the consensus among the Hesters was that everyone had the right to do it if it felt like the proper thing. Barney told me that every death was a suicide.

"What if your plane crashes?" I asked him.

"Then it's the pilot committing suicide on behalf of the passengers."

"You can't commit suicide for someone else."

"Jesus killed himself."

We went to a Catholic school, so this revelation shocked me. "That's not what Father Brophy says."

"He could've saved himself, but he didn't. That's the definition of suicide."

I let it rest. Barney didn't open up very often, and I didn't want to risk having ants stuffed down the front of my jeans. Barney took off his shirt and used it to peel the squirrel from the pavement. I followed him into the woods. He tossed the roadkill as hard as he could. He said it was embarrassing for the squirrel, with everyone looking at it and commenting about it. He said the squirrel deserved to be away from all those eyes.

●●●

A week later Barney told me about the girl who lived down the street. She was a few years older than us. Barney was smitten with her. He scrawled her name in his notebooks and textbooks. I finally knew why he'd taken such an active interest in washing himself. I was sleeping over at his house one Friday night when he gave me the dirt.

"Her house is around the bend, on the right-hand side," he said. "She has really big tits. Her hair's long and black and stringy, and when she sits on her porch reading a book, she likes to twist the hair with her fingers."

That's all Barney could tell me about her.

I asked him, "Where does she go to school?"

He didn't know.

"Where did she move from?"

He said he hadn't noticed anyone living in that house before; maybe they'd always been there.

I asked him if he'd seen her tits, her actual tits, like through her bedroom window.

He slapped the side of my head for even thinking about her tits.

It became part of our ritual to ride back and forth past her house on our dirt bikes, hoping to catch a glimpse. There was an agreement that if she ever came out, I wouldn't open my mouth. Only Barney could talk to her, and I was to laugh extra hard at anything Barney said.

Most times the house looked uninhabited. Once in a while a light would turn on or off and we would get really excited. Barney would stop his bike and pretend to tie his shoe. The drapes in the front window were always drawn, though, so we only saw shadows inside.

This went on for two months. I didn't see the mystery girl. Not once. Barney said she obviously didn't like me, since she came out of the house "a lot" when I wasn't around. I was ready to give up hope. I'd decided that this girl was nothing more than a fantasy, a diversion Barney had created because I wasn't entertaining enough for him. A snowless December came and went as I tried unsuccessfully to draw Barney into playing Coleco football, hunting birds with our BB guns – anything that didn't involve the dirty gray house at the bottom of the hill.

●●●

In January there was a blizzard, and with the snow came the girl. Her face was bleeding. She was ushered into the Hesters' house by the grotesquely overweight Mr. Hester, who normally filled his custom-made recliner from the moment he came home from the Keebler factory until Mrs. Hester woke him to get into bed. But with the twelve inches of snow came a lot of shoveling, and doctors had told Mr. Hester he needed the exercise.

He burst through the door with Tanya squeezed under his arm, her face squashed against his enormous stomach. I think Mr. Hester was, in his arrested condition of social development, attempting to both console and restrain her. She was squirming. She screamed. She bit his hand. Cursing, he let her go. She ran to me and started shoving, perhaps in her dazed state thinking that I was the one who'd hit her with the rock-filled snowball.

Barney was frozen to his spot on the carpet. I think there were a couple of things going on in his mind at that moment: first, he was paralyzed at the sight of his dream woman standing in his own house; second, he was horrified that it was *me* she was touching, rather than him, albeit in a rude fashion. If Mr. Hester hadn't thrown his bulk between us, I believe Barney would've joined in with Tanya's assault and I wouldn't be here today to tell this story.

The mess got sorted out. Danny was hauled inside by his ear. He was made to apologize, which he grudgingly did, before flipping Tanya the bird as he stepped out the door. Mrs. Hester brought rubbing alcohol and bandages. Tanya snatched these petulantly. She plopped to the carpet and applied them to her cuts.

Barney and I sat motionless at opposite ends of the couch. His rapid blinking and unsteady breath pattern told me that his brain was going into overdrive. He didn't want to look at the fantasy girl, but his eyes, those pea-green things which for so long had only expressed rage and apathy, were pulled to her. He was terrified.

Barney's parents left the room. Tanya took her sweet time swabbing her wounded temple. I felt unable to move or speak. Barney hadn't lied when he'd said she had big breasts; they were gigantic. In fact, her whole body was rather large. If I can tell the truth, I thought she was homely and dumpy. Her hair was like black seaweed. Her nose looked like it'd been pinched into the shape of a shark's dorsal fin. She had unusually long fingers, which she used to tug absentmindedly at her detached earlobes. They were pale, bony fingers. They reminded me of icicles. Judging by the dark ditches beneath her eyes, she hadn't had a good night's sleep in months.

The silence had grown unbearable when Tanya startled us. "What the hell are you looking at?" she asked Barney. I was almost knocked off the couch by the force of her voice.

Before Barney had the chance to answer, Mrs. Hester shocked us all by coming into the room with a tray of hot chocolate. In two years she'd never even offered me a glass of water.

Barney threw me a look that meant I was supposed to help his mother. I obeyed, handing out the mugs before resuming my seat. Mrs. Hester asked Tanya how her head was feeling. Tanya performed a courageous feat. She screwed up her face, distorted it into a queer, mocking grimace, then answered in a perfectly level voice, "Just fine, ma'am. Thanks for the hot chocolate."

I prepared myself for Mrs. Hester's wrath. She was an alcoholic with a mean streak. Although she was blind, she exhibited an impeccable knack for reading intentions behind people's voices, like a dog that smells another dog's shit on the wind. It wouldn't have surprised me if she'd hurled the tray at the wall and gone rabid on Tanya's ass. Instead, Mrs. Hester simply said, "You're welcome," and walked away.

● ● ●

After that, Tanya began coming over regularly. Barney had promised her that we'd "fuck Danny up" for the snowball.

The three of us spent hours in the back yard, huddled over a floor plan of the Hesters' home that we'd scrawled into the snow. I realized in those moments that three is a good number. In a group of three, you are always next to everyone. It's a perfect circle. (That's why Margaret and I have only one child. He's a five-year-old boy. I wanted to call him Barney, but that would have upset Margaret. So we named him Evan. Barney is his middle name.)

Our idea was to put headphones on Danny while he was asleep, then destroy his eardrums with his own music. We had talked about putting dog poop on his floor. We'd considered shoving broken glass into his tube socks. A floor plan wasn't necessary for any of the ideas we tossed around, but Barney was a detail-driven boy, and I wasn't about to argue with him. The true joy of those nights was huddling together against the whipping, frozen breeze, flashlights in hand, watching our breath clouds mingle above the crude snow-sketch, our knees touching.

The actual execution of the plan was anticlimactic. Since we had to wait until Danny was sleeping, we chose a Friday. I spent the night at the Hesters'. We told his mother we were going to sleep in the basement living room, which was next to Danny's room and which also had a sliding glass door leading into the backyard. In front of the television Barney and I lay in our sleeping bags. Barney stuffed handful upon handful of Cheetos into his mouth.

Barney's teeth were bright orange when Tanya's face appeared in all its bloodless glory at the glass door. Barney let her in. It was 2:00 A.M.

We took turns sneaking to Danny's door and pressing ears against it. We had to flatten our entire ear on the door for ten seconds or it didn't count. This was terrifying, knowing that Danny could whip open the door at any moment and then do God-knows-what. He was like an ogre in a cave.

After two turns apiece, we determined that he was asleep. The mood turned solemn. We snuck into his room with a flashlight. Barney selected AC/DC's *Back in Black* from the leaning stack of records, and I plugged in the headphones. Tanya had insisted on the privilege of placing the headphones over Danny's ears. As soon as she did, however, he woke up. Barney didn't even get a chance to drop the needle before Danny flung back his covers and started screaming obscenities at us. He leapt from his bed. Tanya kicked him in the shin with her boot. She ran out of the house, leaving the sliding door wide open. The breeze played on the curtains and stirred up the newspaper that was lying on the sofa. Danny punched Barney a few times in the mouth. That was that.

●●●

If Tanya had ever been interested in Barney, which I doubt, she lost interest after that night. That's not to say she didn't come over anymore. She did. The three of us took long walks through the woods. We shot BB guns at birds. We threw snowballs at cars on the Beltline. Despite her rotund figure, Tanya proved to be a remarkably fast runner. She had a natural gift for vanishing into the trees, making no sound whatsoever. Whenever a car skidded to a stop and the driver hopped out to chase us, Tanya became a blur, sprinting smoothly over snow mounds and dead branches, through bushes and fallen saplings, until inevitably she was gone, only to announce her appearance later, when the coast was clear, by pelting Barney in the face with a snowball.

Barney took these assaults, as well as others, as signs of affection. How could he not? He was blinded and weak. Love to Barney meant punching, spitting, and ignoring. But I sensed different motives in Tanya. After all, she never spoke to Barney – only to me. When she spit grape seeds at him or thrust her smelly feet in his face, it was with a malevolence I couldn't ignore. For his part, Barney was so smitten that he could barely talk. So I was constantly in the middle. They talked to me, but never to each other.

Tanya and I were occasionally left alone together. Tanya took these opportunities to criticize Barney's clothes, his hair, his house – anything she could think of. Because she always whispered these derisions, it imbued them with a sense of urgency and secrecy. Her lips curled into a grin. She dripped profanities from her mouth like molasses. Her eyes moved in her head, glancing to the left and right as if she could sense the presence of another being in the room. I became steadily more focused on her breasts as the days went by. When her fingers wrapped around a throw pillow, I imagined she was grabbing my hands, my head, my shoulders – anything – to pull me in for a taste of her moist lips.

●●●

Recently, I was downtown for the annual Thanksgiving parade when I bumped into Danny Hester. He was alone, staring at the newspaper machine. I was reminded of Barney, years before, mysteriously contemplative, hands in his pockets, looking down at the road-kill squirrel.

With my son Evan in tow, I tried to hurry past. Danny looked up. He recognized me. I hadn't seen him in eighteen years. Except for the added age lines, his face was mostly unchanged, but he seemed to have shrunk. And he wasn't Danny anymore, he was –

"Daniel." He shook my hand vigorously. "You know...your brother-in-law?" He looked peculiar in his trench coat and three-piece suit. He didn't ask about Margaret, but he did tell me that Mrs. Hester had "kicked the bucket six months ago" from a stroke. The unspoken message, of course, was that I should pass along the news to Margaret.

For whatever reason – reluctance to get involved in family matters, residual fears of an ass-kicking – I didn't mention that Margaret already knew about her mother's death. She'd seen it in the paper and had grieved privately, in her own way. Margaret had divorced herself from them eight years before, and the Hesters seemed to accept this reality in the same way they'd accepted Uncle Lincoln's suicide: It was unfortunate, but unchangeable. If I'm honest, my attitude wasn't far from theirs. I'd never pressed Margaret on why, exactly, she'd estranged herself. After all, did I need more fuel for my hatred of the Hesters? Did I need to claw open whatever psychic scabs my wife still bore, just for my own satisfaction?

I expressed my condolences to Danny. I told him Margaret would be devastated.

He smiled at my son, rubbed Evan's head. I could practically hear the violins as he broke into a sappy, rambling speech about the old days. It was pathetic. He said he felt like crap the way he'd treated Barney when they were boys. He said that Barney had talked about me all the time, even when we weren't friends anymore. Looking at my watch, I mumbled something about taking my son to the movies. Danny shook my hand again, not wanting to let me go. I peeled myself away.

After walking a few steps, I heard him call after me. I turned around. He said that he'd heard something about Tanya. She'd migrated west, to California, to be an actress, leaving bits of Barney, I presume, in toilets all across the USA.

Now I suppose I should get to the point. My therapists have always told me that writing things down is a way to finalize, to purge, to mend.

●●●

One Saturday afternoon at the beginning of April, Barney's parents announced that it was time to buy the family some new church shoes. Amid protests, they corralled the children. Surprisingly, Mr. Hester offered to drop me off at my house on the way to the mall. (Usually they left me to fend for myself.)

As we all fought our way into the pumpkin-colored station wagon, Tanya materialized on their doorstep. Mr. Hester, trying to be polite, invited her along. She refused with a simple shake of the head. She walked to the car, grabbed me by the arm, and pulled me out.

"I need help," she whispered. Her fingers were crushing my humerus.

"They're giving me a ride home," I said, with the inflected meekness I'd adopted in her presence. Whenever possible, I did what Tanya commanded. I'd once seen her pull off the head of a dead crow we found in the woods. She took it home to use its beak as a "pen" for her diary.

"My parents can give you a ride," she insisted.

The whole Hester family was listening to our exchange as the car idled. Barney wasn't only listening, of course. He was glaring. I tried to pull away, but her icicle fingers wouldn't break.

I relinquished. "I'm going to stay and help Tanya," I said. I stared at the ground, not wanting to make eye contact with anyone.

Mr. Hester spat a vindictive looger onto the driveway and backed the car into the road. He didn't like Tanya. Nobody did except Barney.

She led me to the rear of the Hester house. I didn't know what she had in mind, but all possible scenarios seemed both repellent and alluring. She jimmied open the window to the utility room. She boosted me. I climbed inside. She followed. While I brushed myself off I asked her why we were breaking into Barney's house. As an answer, she ran into the next room. I followed.

For two hours, we wreaked havoc on their home. From the refrigerator we retrieved an onion. We broke off chunks and planted them everywhere – in the teakettle, under the plastic placemats, inside the bottle of dish soap, in the cookie jar. We dumped honey into the coffee maker. We taped together pages of the Merck Manual of Medical Information. We diluted their mayonnaise with Vaseline. We greased doorknobs with butter. As we did these things, we giggled uncontrollably. There was no talking, only giggling. I was delirious, and I couldn't figure out why. Perhaps it was the freedom of running rampant in this house where'd I'd spent so much time being reserved and polite, constantly afraid.

Soon after our orgy of what she called "subliminal vandalism," Tanya took me to the living room. As I settled into the sofa, I calmed down, with the prospect of the Hesters' return heavy in my mind. I told Tanya that we should leave. She pinned me to the couch. She sat on me. She took off her shirt and in a marvelous burst of blubbery flesh unleashed her breasts. She commanded me to kiss them. I obeyed, pecking like a bird at the strange pliable mounds, avoiding the nipples at all costs.

She grew impatient: "Put them in your mouth."

I opened up as much as I could. Neither of them would fit, but I tried. Now and then I glanced up at Tanya. She was staring down at me, her chin doubled, tripled, giving her throat the look of two smiling mouths stacked upon each other. She watched me without joy, as if I was a suckerfish cleaning algae from the fish tank glass. For a few moments nothing existed but those vast pale mammaries and the looming face above.

I think she knew the Hesters would be coming back soon. And even though my therapist has repeatedly told me that attributing supernatural powers to Tanya is nothing more than a defense mechanism, I also believe, deep down, that Tanya knew Barney would be the first to open the door (using his mother's key), and that he would do everything in his power to usher us out before the rest of his family could see what we'd been doing.

That's exactly what happened. Barney came in. He saw us. His face deflated. Without hesitation, without a word, he locked and bolted the front door. Danny started pounding on it. Tanya slipped into her shirt, and we all walked hastily to the back door. Tanya, I remember, was laughing. I was stunned and ashamed, but more so I was terrified that Barney would murder me. Instead, he shoved me out of the house and out of his life.

●●●

I've never told Margaret, or my therapist, any of this. Margaret believes that my absence from her home for those eighteen months was a result of my parents prohibiting me from being with Barney. That's what Barney had told his family. He needed to save face, and so did I.

I stayed far away. The summer passed. I dreamed of Tanya many times. They were nice dreams, dreams of vulgar, sloppy kisses, of hands entwined so tightly they became one piece of flesh. Later, the nature of my Tanya dreams changed, but the dreams began that summer.

I missed Barney. The look on his face as he'd escorted me out the door – the confusion, his eyes quivering with rage and pain – haunted me. I wanted to hang myself. Barney had been my only close friend. I stayed home on Friday nights. I read my comic books, rode my bicycle around my neighborhood, stared out my window.

When sixth grade began, my pain worsened. Being in the same classroom with Barney, and being ignored by him, was almost intolerable. He never looked at me, spoke to me, or referred to me in conversations with other people. In his eyes, I'd vanished. I got used to it eventually – I had to – by buddying up with the class reject, "Stinky Harold" Trebek. Barney went out for all the sports – baseball, football, basketball, and even track – so by default I had to drop those activities.

My parents were concerned about me. I was growing taller, but my weight wasn't keeping up with my height. My appetite shrank until I was only eating from necessity. My entire life philosophy changed in those eighteen months. Sports no longer interested me. Deciding to devote my future to veterinary medicine, I took up collecting wild animal cards with fervency. I experienced the first uncomfortable pangs of doubt in the existence of God.

●●●

When seventh grade rolled around, I was totally alone. Stinky Harold had moved away the previous summer, so I became the class reject. The other boys sported acne and dirty mustaches and squeaked when they laughed. I was taller, but otherwise externally unchanged. Friendship seemed an investment I couldn't afford to make.

I should probably be grateful for those solitary months. During that time my thoughts inexplicably turned to Barney's sister Margaret. I realized that she'd always been there, on the periphery, a quiet, soothing presence in the chaos of that unsettled home. She had smiled at me when no one else would. She had a pretty face. Her eyes, I discovered in my reminiscing, had often lingered on my face, but I'd ignored it. Tanya faded from my dreams, and Margaret stepped into the vacancy. I fantasized about calling her. I even dialed their house a few times, only to hang up when Danny or Barney answered.

Then, for reasons I've since figured out, Barney returned into my life.

It began with an invitation, a red sheet of construction paper slipped into my desk. I still have it here in my Barney scrapbook. He wrote, and I quote: *You are invited too selebrate the 12fth berth day of Barney James Hester, on this Saturday at 7pm. Pleese bring a presint for him.*

There was no name on the abominably-spelled document. I thought it had to be a mistake, possibly a joke.

Barney approached me the next day as I stood at the urinal in the boys' bathroom. His first words to me in almost two years were, "Draining the lizard, huh?"

He seemed jovial. I detected no malice in his tone. I was thrilled and nervous at the prospect of forgiveness, but the past eighteen months felt like too enormous a chasm to bridge during a toilet break.

He asked if I was coming to his party. I said I didn't know. He frowned. He said that it was going to be a blast; his parents were buying him a ColecoVision that he didn't have to share with Danny. There was going to be pizza from Fred's, the best in town. He was vague when I asked who else was coming to the party. At last I promised that I would be there. Even after eighteen months apart, I couldn't say no to Barney.

•••

My mother dropped me off. I told her I would catch a ride home from one of the other kids. With present in hand, I paused in front of the unremarkable Hester home. For some reason, I expected it to have changed after such a long absence. After all, I was different, Barney was different, the world was different. The house was the same.

Danny opened the door. Out of habit I tensed up, expecting at the very least a scathing insult. He let me inside without even a nod of his head. He was sullen and quiet, I soon realized, because Mrs. Hester was in the middle of one of her notorious alcohol-induced cleaning frenzies.

For a drunken blind woman she navigated the room with remarkable precision, sweating, hauling the vacuum to and fro, cursing under her breath, dusting shelves, polishing windows. She glanced up when I came in. "Who is that?" she asked, not attempting to hide her annoyance. "Who's in my house?" Danny tiptoed away.

"It's Earl Brinkman," I said.

"You're the one who spit on my carpet, aren't you?" she snapped. "You gonna apologize for that?"

"I'm here for Barney's birthday party," I said. I couldn't recall ever spitting on her carpet, but I wasn't about to argue. "He told me seven o'clock." For once I felt afraid because Danny had *left* the room.

"There's no goddamn party," she said.

I was turning to leave when Barney appeared. He motioned for me to follow. I followed. Mrs. Hester forgot about me and resumed scrubbing the baseboards.

In the basement we plopped in front of the television. No other kids were there. Danny came out of his room wearing his black Cain's Karate jacket and white karate pants. Before leaving for his lesson, he reminded us not to go into his fucking bedroom. I'd forgotten how much I hated Barney's family.

"Where's my present?" Barney asked.

I handed him the package. He opened it. It was a pair of walkie-talkies. I'd chosen these over anything else because they implied that we would use them together.

"We can go hunting," I said. "Like we're soldiers or something."

"Let's do it," he said.

We grabbed his guns and headed out. He carried the powerful ten-pump Ryder pellet gun, while I received the one-pump Daisy air rifle. I never asked about the absence of other kids. I was elated by the notion that Barney had selected me as his sole party buddy. I was his best friend again.

That feeling lasted approximately thirty minutes. Walkie-talkies in hand, we split up. The sun was disappearing. The world dimmed by the minute. I tromped through the woods, heading east, scanning the leafless branches for movement. I received a transmission.

"Nothing over here," Barney's voice said. "Over."

"Same with me," I said. "Over."

I wandered through a dense patch of trees until I reached a small clearing. The woods seemed completely vacant of life. I fired at a log. I pulled the walkie-talkie out of my jacket pocket.

"Where are you?" I said. "This sucks."

"I think I see something," his crackling voice whispered. "I'm getting closer."

I heard the snap of a branch. I turned. I strained my eyes before realizing that Barney was squatting behind a tree at the edge of the clearing, less than thirty feet away. He was aiming his rifle at me.

The gun cracked, followed by an intense stinging in my left hand. I dropped my gun. I ran. Barney chased. I could hear his footsteps crashing. He pumped his gun, and I counted along with it. When I reached ten, I covered my head. He fired again.

I dashed through the clearing, arms and legs ablaze with adrenaline. I arrived in another stand of trees. One of his pellets broke a twig near my shoulder. He kept calling out the same phrase, "I'm gonna get you!" He shouted playfully, as if this was an old game between pals.

My only thought was that I should get to somebody's house, anybody's. He would never shoot me if other people were around. In my disoriented state I didn't know whose house I was approaching when I finally climbed out of the woods.

Tanya was seated atop the picnic table, staring into the trees as if expecting me to emerge. Up the sloping backyard I ran to her.

"Help," I said. "Barney's after me."

"Oh, he is?" she said. There was something strangely theatrical, even by her standards, in her voice. I've played it over enough in my mind to know. "Well, let's just see about that."

Barney came stomping onto her lawn. He was winded, pale, and disheveled. This is how I remember him. He pumped his gun with cool deliberation, adding his own element of drama to the scene. It was too unreal for me. I hid under the picnic table.

Peeking through my fingers, I saw it unfold. I will tell you what happened.

Tanya walked forward. Barney walked forward. They were like gunslingers. I couldn't see Barney's face. Tanya in her dirty blue jeans started to skip in a circle, singing a song: "Barney, Barney, you forgot your hat. Barney, Barney, you'll pay for that."

"Get out of the way," Barney said. His voice was tiny. "Or you'll get it right between the eyes."

"Barney, Barney," she said. She wasn't singing anymore. "Give me the gun."

The next thing I knew, the gun was hurled into the air. It landed with a crash on top of the picnic table. I recoiled at the noise.

When I looked up again, Tanya and Barney appeared to be engaged in a peculiar dance. With her hands on his shoulders she pranced around him, chanting "Barney, Barney," over and over. He was motionless; his shoulders slumped. He gazed directly at me. The way his eyes looked at that moment has never left my mind: helplessness, surrender, blame. All at once he worked himself into a plaintive wail, that carnival shriek. His head vanished into her mouth, followed by his neck, arms, Detroit Lions jersey, parachute pants, and blue Converse sneakers.

That's all I can see. The rest is buried.

● ● ●

I was repacking the Barney Box yesterday, preparing it for the trip to the garbage dump. It's got a few of his pocket combs (some with strands of hair still intact), the old hand-held football game, photographs, school notebooks, the birthday party invitation. Even his pellet gun is in there. It took a few years to get this stuff back from the Grand Rapids Bureau of Missing Persons, and it still retains the musty odor it acquired there.

I couldn't bring myself to throw everything away. Reliving that period of my life during these past few months has brought it close once again. Yesterday while Margaret was at work, I peeled through the box in search of the walkie-talkies. For some reason it seemed appropriate to keep these, although I wasn't sure if they still worked.

I could only find one of them. I searched through the box a second time, taking everything out, without any luck. Confused, I sat at my desk with the walkie-talkie in hand. I stared at it. It felt as if everything I'd said to Barney, everything he'd said to me, was contained in that tiny piece of plastic. For the hell of it, I pressed the button.

"Earl to Barney," I said. "Come in, Barney."

A few seconds passed. I was about to toss the thing in the box when, in my hand, the walkie-talkie came to life with a loud crackle.

"I'm here," a voice said.

I dropped the radio onto the hardwood floor. My body trembled uncontrollably. I told myself that I'd imagined the voice because there was no other explanation. If he was calling from the Other Side, then I didn't want to speak to him. My life was complicated enough. I wondered if he'd been swallowed with his walkie-talkie in his pocket. I wondered if Barney Hester had been frozen in time, perpetually twelve years old, all these years just waiting for my call, clutching his radio, praying to be contacted by his only friend. I'd never attempted to reach him. In all the years following his disappearance I'd only thought about myself, only thought about what he'd done to me, when all along I'd done nothing for him. I'd betrayed him. He'd been calling out to me in my dreams and my waking thoughts, and I'd never known how to reply.

The door creaked open. My son stood in the hall in his Sponge Bob pajamas. He was holding the other walkie-talkie.

"Why didn't you answer me?" he said.

Eyes

As the bandages were removed from her eyes, she woke into light and shadow.

She saw her fiancé for the first time. A dim room, a face. She saw his features and felt nauseous. His roundness, his cleft chin, his crooked nose and thick eyebrows – why did she want to rip it all to pieces with her fingernails?

Tears spilling, he said, "My baby. Does it hurt?"

Congenital cataracts had robbed her vision at age four, but she was imprinted with three images from those sighted years: A silver wristwatch glinting in the sunlight; a stack of alphabet blocks; a blue jay on a windowsill. She had never known whether they were real, the memories, but they had haunted her darkness for decades.

Her body accepted the transplanted eyes. She found herself staring at lawns and telephone wires. She watched the legs of children swinging in the park. A trance fell upon her. She forgot time until her fiancé whispered, "We should go."

For his birthday, she gave him a silver wristwatch. They ate lunch on the patio. The sun struck the watch face and caused a bright flash. She set down her napkin and, not letting her fiancé see her tears, went inside.

He didn't know about the images. She wanted to tell him, but she knew it would be a mistake. Hiding the truth was the natural thing.

When she purchased a tin of children's blocks, she said it was to learn the alphabet.

It was true. She still used Braille. Reading was one of many commonplaces she would have to master: primping before a mirror; driving a car; looking into her fiancé's eyes. "Give it time," he said. "I don't mind."

While he was at work, she built a tower of blocks in the living room.

Moments later, she boarded a bus to the library and abandoned the tin on a table in the children's area.

She couldn't explain her reactions to the spark of light, the innocent column – but in both cases, her throat seized. Her chest panicked.

And still, she sought out the final image.

On the internet, she found a photograph of a blue jay. It had no effect.

Mornings, sipping coffee, she stood in slippers on the back lawn. Once, she saw a blue jay on the low branch of a tree. It screamed at her and flapped away.

As months passed, she saw hundreds of jays. Never on a windowsill. Through binoculars she peered at neighbors' homes. She watched nature shows. She hung birdfeeders outside the kitchen, the bedroom.

She tried to swallow life with her eyes, but it felt like the opposite.

One day she married, and another day, she bore a baby boy.

And sometimes, in the gray light, she studied her husband as he slept, loving him for what he would never know.

Hand

None of this was little brother's choice. The emptiness beside the ghost was the only open seat on the school bus.

He could hear the older boys chanting: *Ghost. Ghost.*

He hugged his backpack and sat. Taller by a head, the ghost drooled onto her sweater, watering a rose that resided there.

Far away, at the back, big brother made the older boys laugh.

•••

Every morning, little brother flanked her. His body jostled with the movement of the bus. On the sixth day, he felt brave. He snuck glances. Her skin was chalk. Nose chapped and hooked. Orange hair draped her shoulders. No lips. A bloated, featherless bird. A familiar odor issued from her body, pleasant and ripe, a smell that tucked little brother into dreams of being pierced and lifted by talons.

When he awoke, he checked beneath his shirt. No stomach holes, only dissatisfaction and dread as the bus arrived, brakes screaming.

•••

A week later, the ghost opened her mouth.

Bumpy ride, bumpy ride. Aren't you glad that we're inside? Aren't you glad nobody died?

She was singing.

•••

Physically, she was eleven. Maybe twelve. Maybe a teenager. The kids knew only that she wasn't smart. She never closed her mouth, but she rarely spoke. She couldn't write her name – couldn't, perhaps, dress herself. She wasn't a ghost; her pale complexion was all it had taken.

However, she levitated. Glancing to be certain no one was looking, her body rose six inches off the bus seat, a cautious balloon. Her cheeks flushed red, blue, and yellow; lights underneath her skin. Down she came, smiling. She touched a finger to her nose and winked.

• • •

He saw her in the halls, on the playground, in the cafeteria. He was afraid to approach, flanked as she was by bigger children. Red-faced, cruel, they danced around her until chased off by grown-ups.

Only on the bus in the mornings was the ghost there like breath, waiting for him even though they never spoke.

He wanted to ask how she ignored their spitting, why she didn't fly away to live on a cloud. But then he pictured his father guarding the water treatment facility, climbing into bed every day as the sun rose. He pictured his mother, slathering bread slices with red jam: *Don't be a coward. Everyone goes to school.* He pictured big brother twisting his ear, imitating the father, delighting in the way the cartilage folded.

• • •

One morning, she held his hand. She was shy, cupping a robin's egg.

The next day, she was bold. She grabbed his hand when he sat down.

Her grip was strong. Sweat mingled. He absorbed the painful joy by ascending through the ceiling. Borne on a weightless wind, he gazed down at the yellow bus as it crawled along the street. The world shrinking, he became a balloon. He drifted into clouds. He searched for her there.

• • •

She reeks, big brother said. Now your hand reeks.

He scratched big brother's face. The mother sent him to his room.

In the darkness, little brother sniffed his hand.

Outside the bedroom, the mother reassured the father. *It's what boys do. No reason to get upset.*

• • •

Big brother demanded little brother stop sitting with her.

Her mom is nuts, he said, and the ghost is retarded. My friends think I like her. They stole my shoes.

Big brother has a few points, the mother agreed. Her lips smacked at her tuna casserole. For the third time today her makeup had been applied, thus the care inserting bites and pressing a wineglass to her lips.

For the father, eating was not to be interrupted. Boys and mother were surprised when he spoke:

There's a genetic component to craziness, he nodded. The jutting Adam's apple above his unbuttoned collar looked like a rock he'd tried to swallow. *Want to know what's wrong with the kid? Check the parent*, he said.

I suppose I could drive him to school, the mother suggested, in a pillowy voice.

The father growled into his can of beer: There's a direct way that doesn't involve acting like a coward.

• • •

The ghost wasn't on the bus the next day. Or the next. Or the next. Little brother took his regular seat. In his mind, she touched him, and her songs lived like worms.

The other children pointed at the emptiness beside little brother. Now she really *is* a ghost, they said.

• • •

One night, little brother awoke. The ceiling crawled with dark continents. He thrashed in his bed, feverish. The ghost knelt at his side, molding his hand like clay. *I'm making a bird that looks like me,* she said.

Then she became the father, unsmiling as he manipulated little brother's hand. Little brother walked backwards into sleep. *Out of the dream,* he thought. *I am backing out of this dream.*

In the morning, his fingers were jointless. His left palm was swollen, and together with his unbendable fingers, it crowned his forearm like a deformed flower.

The hand was hideous and itchy. The aroma was of something pulled from the earth. He wrapped the hand in a bandage and told his family he had burned it.

When, exactly? The mother frowned, sniffing the air. She knew everything about her boys, or thought she should.

How does a kid who never touches anything get a burn on his hand? the father mused.

He's full of it, big brother said, sneering across the table. *Unwrap it for us.*

We're going to be late, little brother said. His heart, his ribs; labored breathing like climbing flights. There was a fire in the bones of his hand.

It hurts, little brother whispered. He'd thought he could keep it to himself, but the pain was too much. Tears drew lines down his cheeks. The world turned mouse-colored and blurry. He felt himself fall.

●●●

How long he slept he didn't know. He tried to raise his head. At the end of his arm was a great flesh suitcase, pores wider than pinheads. The hand occupied an entire coffee table next to his bed.

It's wiggling, he said. His raspy voice came from outside his body, from the darkness. The drawn shades stood hot and unmoved.

I know what you mean, the mother answered with a laugh. *But it's a she, not an it.* The mother's complicated gaze fell on him. Forlorn. Smitten. Hateful.

Is it the ghost? he whispered.

Yes, a man answered. Doctor Foster materialized from a corner, his bald head alive with sweat. He dried it with a forearm. *Of course it's the girl. Curled up all snug and tight. Like she was swallowed by a snake.* He and the mother laughed and exchanged a look.

Don't play dumb, the father said to his son. He sat against the dresser, smoking. *You know goddamn well why she's in there.*

Charlie, please, the mother said.

●●●

Little brother lay in bed for weeks. His parents withdrew him from school.

Nights, little brother hummed her songs, trying to remember the words. The ghost was fading from his mind.

●●●

Every morning, he heard big brother preparing for school, heard the mother handing out lunch, kissing a cheek. Little brother lived in fitful sleep.

Minutes or hours later, his father entered and crawled beneath a ragged blanket on the floor.

Why don't you come clean? the father said. He dragged on his Camel and exhaled a smoky cone. What's the point of lying? he continued. Everyone knows you fell in love. You let her in. You aren't protecting anyone.

The hand was not a hand. It was enormous. It was a sleeping-bag housing a full-grown adolescent. The outline of her hips was plain under the skin, her arms nested against her sides, the bumps of her ankles, the individual toes. The rise and fall of her breathing.

●●●

Nights, the father talked.

You confuse me. Blond hair and glasses. I used to ask your mother if you were mine. It didn't matter so much when you were little. What did I care? I said: Let him sing all the stupid songs he wants. Let him finger-paint and feed every baby bird in the neighborhood. But you're in school now, buster. Are you stupid? Those kids will eat you alive. When you grow up, the adults will do the same. So yes. I admit it. I did this to you. I don't regret it. Your brother helped. We made this happen. There's a lot you don't know about me, and maybe you need to think about this fact as it relates to everyone in your family. Anyway, you wanted her, you got her. Crap in a pan, you eat it.

●●●

When the ghost was born, nighttime was speaking. Sounds sifted through the window – a bark; a car horn; a triangle of wind chimes.

The hand swelled and kicked. The six feet of skin was an ocean, undulating. The ghost thrashed. Tissue and blood squelched like mouths kissing. A small rip in the skin became larger, a circle.

The father sat against the dresser. Moonlight blued his face. A Louisville Slugger rested on his lap. He'd sent big brother and the mother away. Three days, four nights at a hotel on the lake. He'd drained the bank account so he could be here alone when the ghost was born.

He heard the noise of birth and laid out the facts: I'm going to crush her skull. No questions. You're going to know what disappointment feels like. Why am I warning you? Here's the answer: so you can know what it feels like to know that disappointment is coming but can't do anything to stop it. Two lessons for the price of one.

An hour later, there was a gush of clear fluid as the ghost spilled onto the carpet.

Songless, white, and naked, she sobbed. Her skin trembled. Her throat was clogged with viscous body.

Little brother lacked the strength to lift his head. He was also too afraid to look.

He winced as the muffled cracks resounded.

Dull thumps rejoiced in rhythm, like a heartbeat.

Eventually, the bat broke. The father tossed the handle onto the glistening corpse and then sat down on the floor to catch his breath.

Silence settled on the room. Little brother's body relaxed. His hand lay ripped and splayed across the coffee table. No pain. He was aware that the hand was useless now and would be removed. He wasn't sad. It was relief that he felt. The relief was unexpected. It crouched in his stomach like a new animal.

Unexpected, too, was the father, blood-dotted, crawling to little brother's side and assuring him that the ghost would return. His eyes were dark. His breath warmed little brother's cheek.

Headless or bodiless, the father said, *she'll find her way. She'll climb into that other hand.* He touched the blanket and smiled. He appeared to be sincere.

Happy Turkey Day

None of Jonathan Turkey's friends, teachers, or teammates, nor in fact anyone at Cleveland Catholic Central, nor anyone else on Earth (besides Jonathan and his father Winnicott) knows the origin of Jonathan's unusual surname.

Nor, however, would anyone care. They've heard the name shouted through gymnasium loudspeakers, heard it sung in commercials for the Rare Coin Emporium – they've heard it so often that it has no association anymore with the hideous farm animal that people kill, eat, and make wishes on while they break its bones.

•••

Jonathan Turkey would rather not die in an alley behind the Green Top Tavern on a blustery November night, bare-kneed with his Gap jeans bunched around his ankles, while the icy wind wreaks havoc on his boxer-briefs and the inhabitants therein.

Not like this, God, Jonathan prays silently, forced to stare at a stretch of black pavement strewn with lemon rinds and Styrofoam boxes resembling screaming mouths stained by barbecue sauce and bleu cheese dressing. The stench of worried chicken bones and ashy beer fills Jonathan's nose and, in spite of his terror, makes him kind of hungry. Rain begins to fall, first softly, then hard.

•••

The two teenagers, Claude and Jonathan, had passed through the Green Top's back door ten minutes earlier, arm-in-arm like platonic same-sex friends in certain Middle-Eastern countries. Jonathan was laughing abrasively in a sequence of high-pitched toots and caws that sounded (at least to the waitress unlocking her car in an IHOP parking lot half a mile away) like a bird being devoured by her tabby. The waitress drove home and found a dead blue jay on her porch, which seemed to prove her theory correct, although, when she really thought about it, it hadn't sounded like a blue jay at all.

●●●

Jonathan is the only child of widowed rare coin dealer Winnicott Turkey. Winnicott is a minor celebrity in Cleveland, a successful businessman who golfs for charity once a year and whose commercial jingle ("Winnie Turkey's Rare Coin Emporium!"), while weak on melody and lazy on lyrics, is ingrained in the mind of any local who watches even a few hours of TV a week.

Jonathan is also Cleveland Catholic Central's finest but most rash-ridden point guard, the winner of two MVP trophies (so far). He possesses the highest per-game rebound average (11) in Cougar history. To sexually-mature CCC junior Gloria Emert (whose parents own a yacht in the Keys and a summer home not far from the Kennedy compound in Hyannis Port) Jonathan is committed boyfriend, prayer partner, and soul mate. He will even mow, for free, your lawn. (If you live within a few blocks and have a physical problem with mowing your own lawn, and if you ask nicely while he's in the presence of his dad. After all, like most of us, Jonathan believes at his core in the value of good deeds, but he often needs a little prompting.)

●●●

When the blade nibbles at his throat, Jonathan envisions pivoting his torso, delivering a simultaneous left forearm sweep/right rib-punch, capturing the knife, and slicing open the belly of the fat gay bastard who is squeezing a fistful of Jonathan's too-long hair.

(Just this morning Dad said, "Cut that mop, boy. You look like a woman." Kneeling in the frigid rain, Jonathan scolds himself: when would he learn that Dad was old and, despite appearances to the contrary, wise? Sure, the Emporium was going down the crapper, and Dad had wrecked the car a couple times. And sure, there was that vial of cocaine in the cookie jar. But hell, even Michael Jordan probably hit a few rough patches on his way to the top.)

The hair-pulling intensifies. Jonathan's face is forced skyward until he's blinded by the flavescent bulb above the tavern's back door.

●●●

The boys met two hours ago, inside the Green Top Tavern. They arrived in separate cars – 2005 Jaguar XJ8, 1996 Ford Taurus. Neither boy was old enough to enter, let alone drink, but the owner/bartender of the cruddy little craphole knew Winnicott Turkey, and therein laid the problem.

●●●

Snugly fitted behind the wheel of his Audi A8 is Winnicott Turkey. Warm. Cocooned. Steve Miller on the stereo. Winnie draws a vial from his shirt (careless these days), taps a mound onto his palm, snorts it, closes the vial and re-pockets it. His hands feel dry and itchy. The Green Top Tavern, blurred by the pouring rain, waits beyond his windshield. He is here to get $1300 from the retarded bartender. Two hours ago, he received a phone message. The voice was obvious even after so long. The money had been a loan for the down payment because Betsy was barely underground when Winnie felt the urgent need to get this bar out of the Turkey family's hands, no matter what the cost.

The Rare Coin Emporium that Serjo ("Joe" after 1955) lovingly bequeathed before his death has gradually become a husk of the empire Winnicott (yes, Winnicott, not Joe) built. Now it is merely a means of sustaining a drug habit. His house has been mortgaged twice. The Visa Exec, AmEx Titanium, and MasterCard Diamond are maxed out. Last summer, repo men hitched a tugboat to *What's Next* while he and the kids were pulling up to the dock after a Lake Michigan cruise. In a panic, embarrassed, he'd told Johnny and Gloria that he donated the sailboat to a poor family. To be laughed at by his own son! And what kind of laugh was that, anyway? In his generation you could read a person's laugh, but kids nowadays had thirty different ones for every occasion. In so many ways, Johnny had become like a foreigner – the odd odors, the bizarre language, the demanding and sneaky attitude. Like a beaten seal, that laugh.

● ● ●

Claude Poopdick (Peuptic, really, but you know how nicknames go) grips the stumpy rope of hair and eases Jonathan's face toward the yellow light. Claude yanks, but sadly gets neither scream nor squeal: Turkey barely grunts. Or maybe doesn't grunt at all. The rain is noisy as hell.

Claude never counted on cacophonous rain. How can a prisoner be tormented effectively, Claude wonders, when the tormenter can't hear the prisoner's reactions? The situation is starting to feel like one of God's fucked-up tricks, and it sends Claude into a quiet rage, which is his preferred kind of rage, one he has practiced for many years and which he will now, he promises himself, at last take advantage of.

He draws a deep breath before hissing, "Are you scared? Are you afraid to die?"

Before he utters these taunts, Claude imagines they'll sound explosive, unbalanced, frightening. But spoken aloud now they seem like the prissy inquisitions of a 5-year-old. Claude's are helpless, puppy-born-without-legs questions that invite answers, which is not, Claude knows, the way to terrorize. But then Claude, with relief, considers that

Jonathan was unable (perhaps) to actually hear the questions. The rain rattles the tops of the garbage cans.

(Claude is petrified of death. "To lie in cold obstruction, and to rot" – he is haunted by this Shakespeare line from last year's English class. The line is a part of him now; he'd like to forget it, but he can't, any more than he can forget his feet. Every few days, he fends off a bout of dizziness when bulldozed by the realization that the shell of a body that is "him" will someday be rotting underground while his mind, his essence, will be sucked into crushing dark space forever. The world he knows won't exist. He will metamorphose, like a character in a fairy tale, into a series of lines carved into a granite slab, lines forming the nonsensical phrase "Claude Peuptic." Claude draws deep, concentrated breaths when the terror strikes; supine on the couch, he digests the white ceiling with his eyes and uses his fingers to count his pubic hairs. This distracts him well enough.)

● ● ●

Winnicott Turkey hates himself. He has misdiagnosed his self-hatred, however, as self-pity, and so he does everything possible to eliminate self-pity from his life. Thus, when choking the throat of his popular and sport-gifted son, Winnicott translates this as the compulsion to murder his offspring so that others will feel sorry for him like they did three years ago. He desires others' pity so he won't need his own. For this same reason, Winnicott crashes BMWs into trees; he drives the family business into the ground; he blows $1100 a week on blow. His efforts to evoke pity leave his self-hatred intact while compelling no one to feel sorry for him.

All of this has something to do with Betsy, but Winnicott is never sober long enough to sort out his psychic wounds.

● ● ●

Those who know Jonathan know he is a well-mannered, athletic, attractive teenager with a bright future in politics or law. (He has a 5 – 1 debate team record and gives motivational talks during children's Bible study about the dangers of underage drinking.) Those who know Jonathan also understand that basketball is an epically difficult career to break into, and that a more prudent plan will involve departing the basketball court in favor of an appellate court.

Most of those who know Jonathan don't know about his rashes. These have come and gone since he was twelve, resembling in color the inside of a watermelon and in texture the scales of a snake. Usually it takes less than an hour for the rashes to fade. (Jonathan's mother, before she died three years ago, called them "little sunsets.") Jonathan's main fear is that they will flare up during a game. Word would spread like the rash itself, from person to person, until everyone knew he was a monster.

●●●

Although Claude knows that his surname isn't the *sole* cause of his pariah status at CCC (just as it wasn't the sole cause of the elementary and middle school taunting), there are few moments that pass without wishing he'd been born a respectable Johnson, Stone, Brokaw, or Tucker. Surely that wasn't too much to ask.

As the rain tickles his head and the blade in his impressively rock-steady hand rests dangerously near the jugular of the most popular jock in school, Claude asks himself: "Is it even possible for a 'Claude Peuptic' (or a 'Dick Trickle,' or a 'Shelly Weiderhole,' or a 'Harry Sack') to be well-adjusted?"

And if the answer is "No!" and our lives are so pre-determined by birth names (Claude eases the blade pressure ever-so-slightly from Jonathan's neck), then why is he, Claude, so eager to punish this poor jackass for a God-given chance at mocking an easy target?

In fact, hadn't he, Claude, planned in second grade on assailing Marty Dicker with either "Farty Marty" or "Farty

Stinker" (his indecision had cost him dearly) just before Jonathan's first calls of "Poopy Poopdick!" that forever changed his life? Surely the taunters, in this merciless Darwinian universe of nomination, have as little control as the tauntees.

Except here, right here, soaking and shivering in front of Claude's rage-reddened face, kneels the rebuttal to this idea: Jonathan Turkey. How has this bastard skated through life – always Mr. Popular, Mr. I'm Gonna Bang Whoever I Want At Every Dance? A fowl (ha-ha!) name, and yet no repercussions – from St. Jude's, to Riverside, to Catholic Central, Claude cannot recall a single incident when Jonathan Turkey was treated like anything other than a king.

What angers Claude most, though, even more than the hero worship and the numbness to the moniker, is the utter indifference J.T. and his adoring fans display toward their own mortality. Johnny Turkey is king of the blind, duke of the deluded, emperor of the idiot Adonises who are too busy with proms and pep rallies to notice the wild boar crouching in wait around the corner.

Yes, punishment is long overdue, and no one but Old Poopdick has the balls to pull it off.

●●●

One question eats at Winnicott: Why was Betsy taken? She was friend, partner, mother to his child. Her bone marrow was invaded so fast chemo wasn't even possible. Nothing to do but pop the corn and watch her die. No chance to fight back – the cruelest, most dehumanizing way to go. He felt such sickening impotence during those four months that he resolved (not consciously, but a resolution just the same) to never again go down without swinging.

Winnicott can't understand why she died. Worse, he can't bring himself to try to understand, or even to try to understand his inability to understand. Instead, he pushes the painful question aside whenever it hits. He remains profoundly depressed three years after the fact. The closest he has come to confronting the question was when he speculated that God was trying to humble him for transforming his father's corner concern into a million-dollar enterprise. But Winnicott resisted this conclusion: He hadn't been motivated by greed! This was America, the land that made a rare coin dealer out of a Polack stowaway!

"Why be a man," Serjo used to say, "when you can be a success?"

The line was Bertolt Brecht's, from Dad's prized possession: *One-Liners for a Headliner's Life, Volume XVIII*.

●●●

Jonathan Turkey, on his knees in the rain ten minutes after walking out the back door arm-in-arm with his captor, would like to rend the knife from the fat gay bastard and penetrate deep into the disgusting, pale, blubbery Poopdick poopgut that keeps obscenely bumping Jonathan's left shoulder. Jonathan would like to steal the knife, stab the gut, twist the blade, and unleash a steaming jackpot of red-black blood that spatters the pavement in heavy applause not unlike the crowd that erupts every week when the man in the loudspeaker yells, "JONATHAN TURKEY, POINT GUARD, NUMBER FOHHHRRTEE-TOOOOOO!"

For now, though, Jonathan understands that he must remain calm and motionless. He has seen at least eighty TV shows and movies in which a man undoes his captor with a simple blend of confidence, poise, and physical wickedness. He must concentrate. He must *be* the ball. Or the court. Yes. He is the court on a Sunday morning, gleaming from his waxing, free of footprints; his surface is a mirror; he is a rectangle cradled by bleachers so empty nothing interrupts the column of dust connecting Jonathan to window, window to blue sky, blue sky to God Almighty (and, by extension, to Mom).

●●●

Thirteen-hundred dollars from the retarded bartender is enough for a few eight balls and a couple of hookers, with change for pizza and new basketball sneakers so the boy doesn't think his old man's a total ogre. These are Winnicott's ideas as he watches the world melt on the other side of the Audi windshield. He also thinks about his father.

Under Joe's leadership, the Emporium was a kitten in a top hat. Cute. Not a force to be reckoned with. Dad was too convivial, too imaginative, too tethered to outdated mores. He was fifty-eight when the store opened, an affable buffoon without an entrepreneurial bone in his body. Winnicott was an infant, born to thirty-two year-old Babs. Dad's buffoonery, Winnicott suspects, is what made Babs leave Joe in 1966. Eleven-year-old Winnicott never saw his mommy again.

Dad's favorite Socrates line was, "Rather fail with honor than succeed by fraud." What horseshit! Dad never understood that in America ethics changed with the times, that business and pleasure had cobbled out separate compartments, and that failure – with or without honor – was never an option. To Joe, juggling the coins was more important than display strategy; sipping espresso and doing Lyndon Johnson impersonations trumped the sale itself; instead of upselling, he preferred to "disappear" a 1902 French bullion down his throat, only to pretend, seconds later, to pluck it like a shiny berry from a nearby child's ear. He was a constant irritation to Winnicott, who wanted a father who *earned* respect rather than treating respect as a birthright.

Winnie understands, and appreciates, that Johnny's dedication to *not* joining the family business is ironically the one hope he (Winnicott) has left. Johnny's athletic success is the only way he (Winnicott) can now succeed. The new plan: ride out this year, go to the remaining basketball games, suffer through some dinners with Gloria's parents, line a few pockets (drain the retirement fund, if need be) so that Johnny gets a full ride at a reputable university; and then, clandestinely, check into rehab before shame showers the Turkey name forever.

As General Patton said: "Success is how high you bounce when you hit bottom."

●●●

When the owner of the Green Top Tavern saw Johnny Turkey stride through the front door, he felt obliged to let Johnny drink whatever he wanted, no questions asked. This wasn't because Ronnie Moe was a devotee of high school basketball (he wasn't), nor because he was both officially and unofficially a moron (he was). The reason was the stride. No one strode into the Green Top. People scuffled, moped, stumbled, or hobbled. So right away Ronnie pegged the kid as someone important, someone cleaner and shinier than everyone else. A few minutes later, the waitress Rachel stepped behind the bar and told Ronnie Moe the kid's name; she recognized him from the papers.

IQ-tested in 1954, Ronnie Moe's score of 68 had earned him a "moron" label. (At that time, "moron" was the scientific term for someone with low, but basically functional, brain power.) As a boy he'd snuck into his parents' room and seen the word stamped in red uppercase letters on the evaluation sheet. When the kids at school, unaware of the IQ test, called him a moron, Ronnie punched their heads with his heavy fists, daring them to say it again. They began to call him Ron, Ronnie, or Ronnie Moe. Ronnie didn't grasp the veiled insult. He felt privileged to be given a nickname and wore it with pride; he liked the way it rolled off his tongue so much more easily than "Lester Gibbard," which was his given name.

(Ronnie Moe's face is flat and round, colored like a slice of ham. His long nose appears to be dripping toward his mouth. His vacant eyes are slits, shadowed by a jutting brow. Girthy arms protrude from his oak-tree torso, which is always clothed in earth-toned flannel. His shirt buttons, upon inspection, seem to tremble, threatening to pop loose at the insistence of his bee-stung pecs. For two decades he loaded office furniture into semis at a Steelcase warehouse, until three years ago when he was fired for slipping pamphlets about the Rapture into the filing cabinets. Only days after losing his job, Ronnie depleted his savings to buy the Green Top from a man desperate to sell because of a "family tragedy." That man was Winnicott Turkey.)

So when Johnny Turkey and the pale, unfit kid with the dyed black bowl cut sat hunched over glasses of Goebel's at the corner table, Ronnie Moe began to worry that this might be the start of a new thing, that Johnny might return every week expecting to booze it up and explore his weirdo dark side. Ronnie Moe worried that the cops would catch wind of the underage drinking. Then he'd be fucked. Shut down. Fined a billion dollars. Sent back to prison and raped nightly by four giant black cocks. Executed with a poison needle and damned to Hell once and for all (where You-Know-Who would certainly be waiting).

(For his part, Jonathan had no knowledge of his father's association with the bartender. Jonathan chose the Green Top as a meeting place for two simple reasons: 1) It was a downtown dive that needed business, so they were unlikely to ask for I.D., and 2) Seeing the name "Green Top" in the phone book had stirred a cloudy and unspecific, although compelling, memory of his mother.)

Ronnie Moe stood over the metal sink, spraying glasses and watching kid dynamo Jonathan Turkey suck down beer with the unknown tubby at the corner table. Maybe tubs was Jonathan's boyfriend. Maybe they needed a place to get drunk so they could park and do disgusting things to each other. The regular third-shifters from Jewel-Osco didn't give two shits about coin collectors or high school hoops, so this bar, Ronnie thought, was the perfect place for rich-kid Johnny to live his double life.

Ronnie Moe snorted, spat into the sink. What would Mister Moneypants Rare Coin Dealer do if he knew that Ronnie Moe knew that Mister Superstar Basketball Boy was playing for the other team?

Maybe Winnicott would say, "I'll forget you owe me thirteen-hundred bucks if you forget my son's a queer. Please. I'll throw in five hundred extra. Whaddya say, buddy?"

The blackmail idea was so perfect, so vividly imagined, that over the next ninety minutes Ronnie Moe came to believe it was destined. He performed his job patiently and properly: at the bequest of Rachel, he filled two more pitchers for Turkey and Tubby; he rinsed ashtrays; he poured whiskey; he dropped cash into the safe at the appointed time; he telephoned Winnicott and left a message: "Ya need to git down here see what I got here for ya. Git this loan thing straight once and for all."

The fat kid put on a jacket; Johnny didn't have one. Ronnie spied as he toweled beer-mug circles off a nearby table. He grimaced when he saw the boys link arms while heading toward the back door. If his shotgun had been within reach, Ronnie would've decorated the walls with their brains.

●●●

Jonathan says the knife is cutting him. He says it's freezing in this rain, and he's prone to pneumonia because of a depleted immune system caused by infant chicken pox. He says he'll give Claude five hundred dollars and won't press charges. (The offer is empty. Squeezing one Benjamin out of his old man lately is more trouble than it's worth – a pittance compared to the glory days. Is it because Jonathan still refuses to join the business? Or has the old man finally given up on him? When he and Winnicott do cross paths – a rare event these days – his father seems to have given up on lots of things, like hair-combing, shaving, clean shirts. Jonathan wonders if all of this is his fault. *But still*, he thinks, *that choking shit is horseshit no matter what I did*.)

Jonathan tells Claude in a stern, unwavering voice: "Five hundred dollars. In your bank account tomorrow morning. Say the word and it's a done deal." He's unnerved at how uncannily he sounds like his father, but he's determined not to come off as a scared little pussy, and his dad is tough if he is anything.

Claude Poopdick doesn't answer. However, the burning pressure from the blade lessens.

Then all at once Claude relinquishes his grip on Jonathan's hair.

Jonathan's head tips downward. His neck is sore. His scalp stings. He tries without success to focus on his hands, which are pale against the black, dimpled concrete. The rain rushes over his cheeks. He's being pissed on by God. God's piss is numbing his skin.

Jonathan creates a new fantasy. He's kneeling on the sideline during a timeout in the regional championship; the rain is his sweat; it's the best game of his career – twenty-two rebounds, ten blocked shots, thirty-seven points, and still a minute left! Gloria Emert, serious girlfriend who he devirginized and then made love to nineteen additional times over the past six months, who has seen his horrible rash (some of it) and doesn't seem to mind, sits in the back row of the bleachers with her mother and younger sister.

Gloria is waving her CCC banner, but she looks troubled. She has never seen Johnny sweat so much. "He needs medical assistance, doesn't he?" she mouths to her mother. Gloria's mother also appears worried, and she answers, "Even young men with no body fat, long penises and otherworldly blue eyes can die of heart attacks, sweetheart."

Gloria fears Johnny's rash: that it will come to life in front of the crowd, spread across his torso like a time-lapse movie of mold on bread. She is worried because then she'll have some explaining to do to her mom and friends. Johnny seems (Gloria seems, with her flexed eyebrows, to think) so frail, so genetically flawed; after all, he's supplicant on his knees; sweat flows over his cheeks; fear and helplessness contort his hair-free, feminine (for now, but [hopefully] blossoming soon into manly) face.

Jonathan raises his eyes to meet Gloria's gaze. He reassures her with his famous dimpled grin that he will survive this trauma and will be so inspired by his survival that he'll comprehend the profundity of life in a way beyond the capabilities of most men his age. He will propose marriage and they'll be engaged for two years, during which he'll accept the Indiana University scholarship, break numerous records, excel at his coursework while helping Gloria complete her Associates from the nearby two-year college, have a long and lusty affair with a Hoosier cheerleader (or two), nobly break off the affair(s) with Gloria none the wiser, get drafted by the Pacers, and put himself, Gloria, and their newborn son Kurt (named after Grandpa) into a 3,000 square foot home overlooking a man-made lake near the Ohio/Indiana border.

●●●

A mint buffalo nickel from the year after Serjo arrived in America – the very year such nickels were minted – will soon be less valuable than a 1978 Meatloaf cassette. Only geriatric men care about rare coins, and they prefer beach-digging to shopping. Or else they bid on the internet, and Winnicott, admittedly, has dropped the ball on the website. Winnicott's desire is gone. He has tried to pass it to his son, but his son didn't want it. No businessman can survive without desire. He realizes this, and it hurts.

Worst of all, father and son don't see each other anymore. They drift along like planets whose orbits converge monthly on the way to the indoor Jacuzzi. He never attends Johnny's games, never asks about Gloria, never teaches his boy about shaving, STDs, or rare coins. When he does see Johnny, out comes the criticism – a lame joke about the shaggy hair, a scolding about the self-help rash CDs – or a mild throttling.

When, Winnicott wonders, did I become a monster?

• • •

The official police report will conclude that no one (miraculously, some say) is to blame; in fact, everyone behaved heroically. Winnicott fired because he thought Ronnie Moe was threatening Johnny. Ronnie Moe pointed his shotgun at Claude because Claude was threatening Johnny, and Ronnie Moe shot his first barrel at Winnicott because in the dark Winnie looked like a psychopath preparing to shoot Johnny. Claude Peuptic, inarguably, menaced Johnny with a knife (so if anyone bears blame, it's Claude), but he redeemed himself by shoving Jonathan out of the way of Ronnie's second barrel (fired in a state of half-dead shock and intended for no one in particular).

• • •

Ronnie Moe stomps toward the back door, the Stevens 411 12-gauge's 28-inch barrel directing him like a divining rod. Punishment and absolution are on his mind. If he can catch the boys in the act and freeze them in position with old "Double-Eye," then Mister Rare Coin Dealer will be able to witness the expensive truth for himself, once he arrives. Ronnie's steps thunder heavily, deliberately, while the rain outside hisses like a hot radiator.

Claude Peuptic stands behind the crouched, waterlogged form of Jonathan Turkey, who turns his head slightly, just enough to reveal, in the bruised light, a face covered by a scaly red rash. It is ghastly. Claude gasps. Embedded like a gemstone in a pile of raw hamburger is an eye, clear and open and glistening, imploring Claude to do his worst.

Jonathan Turkey burns in the cold rain. His doctor has said the rashes are triggered by stress and has prescribed a CD engineered with messages hidden beneath soulless electronic music, messages imploring Jonathan to relax. Is he incapable of relaxing on his own? If so, it's Dad's fault, with his lectures about cost-effectiveness, investment resiliency and profit margins, and how it would be such a slap in the face to poor old Joe if Johnny didn't take over the business.

Winnicott, seated in his Audi, doesn't notice his son's Jaguar parked across the street. He removes the SW99 from the glove box, checks the chamber. The name, he recalls, was Betsy's. "Green top" was what it sounded like Johnny was saying when he said "guitar" as a toddler. It is written in the baby book: "Guitar sounds like 'green top' – funny." The joint was a struggling gay bar when Winnie bought it ten years ago. Betsy wanted to turn it into a jazz club. She was a big music fan. Or else she hated gays. Winnicott can't remember anything about her anymore.

Jonathan won't listen to the CD. Knowing about the subliminal messages changes them, he has argued, into liminal messages, which defeats the whole purpose. Winnicott's answer to this is that he paid an arm and a leg for that goddamn fucking recording and Johnny will listen whether he likes it or not. The way Johnny sees it, it's a battle for his own mind. But now, kneeling in this alleyway, he finds himself willing to relinquish his mind in exchange for the protection of a father.

Claude Peuptic doesn't hate Jonathan Turkey, doesn't in this moment wish him dead. Maybe it's the sight of The Almighty J.T. squatting near so many gnawed chicken bones. Maybe it's the painful-looking rash on Johnny's face, neck, and – yes – arms and hands. Maybe it's their earlier conversation, which culminated in a tipsy, arm-in-arm stroll toward the back door. Whatever the reason, Claude feels his anger peacefully redirecting. What Claude wants now, more than blackmail or blood, is to be renamed, redescribed, reunderstood. Why, Claude wonders, do names have to be verbal at all? Language is a faulty system. His name could be a scent in the air, a taste on the tongue's buds, the flapping of hung sheets undulating in the breeze.

Winnicott sold the bar at a steal to a mentally challenged Bible-thumping ex-con. Days later, he engraved Betsy's maiden name (Forrester), rather than her married name (Turkey), on her tombstone. Johnny hated (still hates?) the latter decision but loved (still loves?) his dad.

Jonathan rises to his feet, turns. He faces Poopdick, faces the butterfly knife. With the plastered black hair and the Molly Hatchet shirt sagging like excess skin from his blobby frame, the real Poopdick has returned. The earlier Poopdick, whose aggressively scrawled, nearly illegible note (by Johnny's reckoning, it read: *Meet me at the venue of your choice, 8PM, ALONE AND AWAY FROM ANYONE WE KNOW Otherwise EVERYONE learns about your RASH!*) penetrated Johnny's locker was not the Poopdick the CCC Senior Class had grown to love. Here again, however, stands the familiar queasy-looking punching bag. And yet, there is an additional attitude residing in Poopdick's eyes. It is unmistakable: pity. Pity for Jonathan.

This ignites a rage like Jonathan has never felt.

Winnicott steps out of his Audi and into the torrent. The cold rain soothes his scalp. He presses the button on his keychain. The *BOIP-OIP!* means the alarm is engaged. He pockets the handgun.

Through the popcorn-popping rain, the *BOIP-OIP!* reaches Jonathan's ear. He recognizes it like a baby duck does its mother's quack. Jonathan makes a spontaneous action-hero decision: to unleash a scream like a woman being torn in two. He screams until his throat shreds while lunging upon Claude Poopdick, knowing that while it can't actually be his father's alarm-engage, whoever the *BOIP-OIP!* belongs to will (hopefully) enter the alley and lend a hand with Claude's ass-whooping.

Ronnie Moe kicks open the back door, shotgun brandished, at the same moment that Winnicott Turkey steps into the neck of the alley, SW99 drawn.

As if a handle has been turned, the downpour becomes a trickle.

All have heard Jonathan's scream.

For Winnicott, it is the scream of a three-year-old who has crashed his bicycle into a tree. A cry echoing all these years but never answered.

For Ronnie Moe, it is the scream of big brother Danny just before the hammer crushes his skull. Would Ronnie take it back if he could? Of course. He was a damn idiot to do it. A big brother can't be killed, not ever.

For Claude, the scream is his own. Not a scream from his mouth, but one he has attempted to sketch in his notebook as a dark, shrouded figure, a personification of the soul agony he feels each day upon waking. (Dramatic? Yes. His response – and he has thought about it – is that his generation needs more drama and less calculated cool.) The de-pantsing and butterfly knife were intended to make Jonathan feel the *reality* of mortality; that Claude has inspired this scream in his archrival means his mission is a resounding success.

Except now Jonathan head butts Claude's solar plexus, leaving Claude gasping. Claude is thrown hard to the pavement. The wrist of Claude's knife-bearing hand is kneeled upon. A rashy hand squeezes Claude's throat.

Jonathan is surprised at how soft Claude's skin feels, how delicate and crushable the windpipe. With Poopdick immobilized, Jonathan turns to see men with guns at six and nine o'clock. South and west. The south one – potentially Dad – is only a silhouette, but a handgun glints. The west one is the bartender, deranged-looking, bearing a shotgun with both barrels directed at Jonathan (or Claude?).

Winnicott stares into the alley and sees the retarded bartender pointing a shotgun at…could that be *Johnny* there on the pavement thirty feet away? Winnicott feels like rubbing his eyes, it is so dreamlike. Is it a trick of the light? Winnicott doesn't wait to find out. He points the gun he has for two years dreamed of firing, the barrel that has more than once found its way into his own mouth. The trigger responds easily, unleashing a cracking report in the ten-foot wide canal.

Ronnie Moe feels a bee sting in his bee-stung right pectoral. He grunts. Looks down at the blackness spreading across his flannel. Looks up at the two boys, one mounted upon the other. The boy on the ground – the one with the knife – is the real penetrator, the corruptor, the Danny. Ronnie looks toward the south end of the alley, where in a band of moonlight Winnicott Turkey grips a smoking gun. All of this in two seconds. Ronnie raises "Double Eye," aims, and removes the top of Winnicott's head. He uses just one barrel.

•••

According to sworn testimony from sole survivor Jonathan – future CCC salutatorian and proprietor of the *Johnny Forrester Rare Sports Memorabilia Hut* – the wounded Lester Gibbard (aka, "Ronnie Moe") collapsed after shooting Winnicott. His shotgun clattered to the cement. Lester lay motionless.

Jonathan then disarmed Claude and helped Claude to his feet. Both boys stood, teeth chattering, in drippy silence. At this point, Jonathan didn't know that his father was dead. Rachel, a Green Top server, attracted by the gunshots, pushed on the back door only to find that Lester Gibbard's giant head prevented it from opening more than two inches.

The nudging of the door upon his cranium caused Lester Gibbard to sit upright, growling "Die, you bastard!" or something along those lines. (It was difficult to decipher since his mouth was blood-filled and he was, scientifically speaking, a moron.) He aimed his shotgun at Jonathan's face. Claude Peuptic, the quiet and antisocial kid who no one thought would ever amount to much, courageously shoved Jonathan out of the way and received the full blast in his chest. Jonathan wrested the gun from Lester Gibbard's now-limp hands so that no more damage could be done. (Which is why

Jonathan's fingerprints are on the barrel, trigger, and stock, in case you were wondering.)

Although not happy with the events themselves, the involved families (i.e., Claude's parents and the CCC faculty and students) will be satisfied with the report.

•••

Why had Claude planned all of this? To humanize himself to the bully.

Claude had garnered his courage, written the note, slipped the note into Jonathan's locker. It was time to expose J.T.'s true nature. One-on-one, would Johnny look Claude in the eye and call him Poopy Poopdick, or would he acknowledge Claude's humanity?

Johnny, to his credit, had done the latter. After a few awkward minutes at the corner table, the fact surfaced that Claude had never intended to blackmail based upon Johnny's *RASH*, but upon Johnny's *NAME*. (Claude's penmanship was horrendous.) Johnny relaxed upon hearing this; he drank beer as Claude talked. While stumbling around the internet, Claude had discovered the story of Merkl Tourkee, a Slovenian immigrant who'd worked as a circus tumbler until an elephant stepped on his legs. Hobbled but not defeated, Merkl had volunteered for the most maligned of duties – the geek – in order to feed wife Hazel and infant son Winnicott. He'd diligently bitten the heads off live chickens until his manager, wanting to distinguish Merkl from all the other geeks on the circuit, had glued feathers, beak, snood, and wattle on Merkl and made him switch to turkeys. Merkl had thereafter (Claude informed Johnny) been known as "Murky the Turkey Cannibal." And Merkl (or so Claude had believed, and loudly proclaimed, on the basis of little more than mouse clicks and hope) was Johnny's paternal grandfather.

Jonathan had listened politely to this bizarre story, this family history that was not at all his family history. Fighting the urge to laugh – partly from the ridiculousness of it all, partly from relief that his rash secret was safe – and the temptation to offer a fact-based rebuttal, he'd instead told Claude that it was all true, shameful and true. As the night wore on and the beer took effect, Jonathan's brotherly affection for the pudgy misfit across the table had grown until he'd sworn to himself, internally, that after this holiday weekend he would pronounce a CCC moratorium on the "Poopdick" nickname. The boys had exited the Green Top arm-in-arm, in a tipsy imitation of Dorothy and the Scarecrow following the yellow brick road, and Johnny had almost opened his mouth to tell Claude about the nickname moratorium. Almost.

(Perplexing to many people is how Claude came up with his version of the Turkey genealogy when it is no secret that Jonathan's paternal grandfather founded the Rare Coin Emporium on State Street in 1955, and that he wasn't Slovenian at all. The simple truth is that Claude paid little attention to anyone but himself.)

●●●

Serjo Kurtey arrived on Ellis Island in 1912 as a stowaway on a whaling boat. Four days into his three-month journey, the cook of the *Niewazne* had discovered the malnourished fifteen-year-old in the storeroom, squatting uncomfortably in the narrow space behind a crate of sausage casings. Instead of being arrested and thrown into the hold to face eventual deportation back to Poland, Serjo managed to earn the status of honorary *Niewazne* crew member, thanks in part to his juggling skills, which the captain described as "Fancy as hell."

When Serjo checked in at Ellis Island, the immigration officer recorded his last name with the "t" and "k" in reversed positions. Serjo didn't mind the mistake; he was just thrilled to be in America. He'd been considering Americanizing his name anyway, and assumed that any mistake by the immigration fellow would naturally err on the side of normalcy to American ears. With an American name he might blend in, find a good-paying job, meet drinking buddies and other amateur magicians like himself. Such a name could even help him bag a wife.

Serjo's parents were dead (house fire the year before) and Serjo was an only child – in fact, he could think of no living relative who would be angered if the Kurtey name disappeared forever from the face of the Earth due to this clerical error. He would start a new life in America, and this name – Turkey – would help him to, as he'd once boasted to Warsaw friends using a newly-mastered English phrase, "climb up the greatness."

Such thoughts ran through Serjo's mind after the immigration officer called out "*Sir-joe Turkey – Poland*!" And the word "turkey" also floated there in the murky pond of eighty-seven words Serjo had memorized from his dog-eared Polish-English dictionary. It seemed a "turkey" was an obscure utensil used in men's shaving, though he couldn't remember for sure. He shook the hand of the immigration fellow, who, flashing bright green eyes and offering a firm, calloused grip, baptized Serjo into American life with a wink.

●●●

Two miles east of the Green Top Tavern, in a rented duplex, the IHOP waitress sleeps comfortably beside her tabby.

Outside under a bush lays a blue jay with a broken neck.

Tomorrow morning, another blue jay, very much alive, will wake the waitress with its chatter only seconds before the *Cleveland Plain Dealer* Thanksgiving edition, the fattest of the year, bearing the headline HAPPY TURKEY DAY! arrives with a slap on the porch.

Face

Another morning, another foggy mind clinging to the silky threads of dream. Daylight merely a hope, an assumption based only on precedent.

The man washed at the sink. He lathered his cheeks and dragged the razor over the skin. He heard a prickly scraping sound as the blade shore the stubble.

The man tried to recall a moment in his life when he wasn't standing at the bathroom mirror. Memories floated like vapors, flickering. Was he a father? Yes, it seemed so. Were his children boys? Girls? Either way they were not here, either moved or dead. Would he see them again? He figured it was a fifty-fifty proposition. Those odds had a nice balance.

Symmetry in the natural order. Day and night. Light and dark. His face. The distance between eyes. Width and length of nostrils. Equality of the lips.

An image. Memory or fantasy? A face, beautiful in its symmetry. His wife? The lovely harmony of her teeth when she smiled, wrinkling her cheeks which in turn wrinkled the skin around her eyes. The connectivity – yes, it had been inscribed upon her features.

The children had hugged and laughed with him. His wife had hugged and laughed with him. He had reciprocated. Theirs had been a world of connection and balance.

He rinsed the remaining lather. He brushed his teeth with a motion that resembled the whorls on his fingerprints.

His life began each morning. Every time he brushed away the dust of sleep, the encroachment of decay.

In the mirror, the man noticed the aberration.

His left eye in the mirrored version – it had scooted or slid, he didn't know. The eye lay centered, socket and all, on his cheek. He tried without success to push the eye back where it had been, where it had resided his entire life. (Unless, perhaps, it had done this before?)

His face no longer resembled his face. Or it looked like his face but a comical or tragic version. A dis-repaired self, one not ready for the stage of life.

The man's nose and mouth had also switched positions. His face appeared to scream without sound. His nostrils flared while shaving lotion burned his nose hairs.

He wondered if he should cry out. He wondered if it would make any difference if he cried out.

Would his wife come rushing up the stairs? Would his children trail behind?

If she flung open the door, what would she see?

Would she be able to mentally reassemble the man's face – the face she had presumably fallen in love with? Would she believe that this man was, indeed, her husband?

Or more likely would the man discover that his wife's own face was now unrecognizable?

Her features would be the same, exactly the same, but out of order. A chaos of identity like a broken vase. Her nose jutting from her temple; eyes looking out from her chin; lips vertical and set where her nose used to be.

And his children would huddle behind her, their faces puzzles unassembled.

Together they would be a collection of strangers frightened.

The man would turn calmly back toward the mirror, flip up his shirt collar and loop his necktie. There would be no reason to panic. This sort of thing was bound to happen eventually.

The family would return to their respective rooms, their private locations in the universe.

The house would remain silent, as it was now and had always been.

And the man would stand at the mirror, securing his tie, waiting for order.

Neck

He: I'm a sick man. A sinner. I've hurt so many. I deserve this, Lord, but please make my suffering stop.

She: carried a bowl of water. She stood at a distance and watched by lantern light as her father yelled into the black shroud of trees.

She: didn't want to go near him even though he needed to drink. His neck as fat and round as durian. His face all sweat and distortion.

His lungs: crackled like the power lines in the village. He was finally asleep. The girl set the bowl on the grass and ran back to the tent.

Her mother: didn't look up when the girl came in. Zip it, she hissed.

The young brother: was also feverish, but his neck was not swollen. The mother held a damp cloth to his forehead.

The jungle: buzzed and screamed.

The daughter: settled into the sleeping bag. I put the water by his cot, she said. She expected her mother to scold her for not making him drink.

The mother: hummed a melody that reminded the daughter of the house in Cleveland.

The daughter: closed her eyes and saw her old bed. Could smell the clean sheets. Could see the checkered quilt, the lime-green walls, the lamp on her dresser shaped like a bouquet of balloons. These pictures overtook her mind and left her breathless. Eleven months in the jungle now. She remembered her Ohio friends. Brynn, Zachary, Winnie.

Names only, not faces. Their faces were gone no matter how hard she tried. She would be ten tomorrow.

Did Dad hurt someone?

The mother: stopped humming. Your father is a Christian.

He said he hurt so many.

The mother: He's burning with fever. Say your prayers and go to sleep.

Is he going to die?

The mother: extinguished the lantern.

The young boy's nose: whistled.

The mother: lay atop her sleeping bag in the dark. Her eyes were open. We're all going to die someday, she said.

Some of the parishioners: had called her father a *cuentero*.

The daughter: wondered if her father had tried to swallow his lies. Maybe they'd gotten stuck in his throat and gathered there, day after day, filling him until his neck became a ball. She wondered if she and her brother and her mother would go home.

The daughter: slept deeply and dreamed of needles popping balloons.

Sores

Jim climbed the carpeted stairs, flipping through the mail, experiencing again the vague hope that something in the stack might provide him a welcome home after his day's work. A letter from an old Grayling buddy? An unexplained check from an unknown source? These fantasies were impossible – the past six months had borne out this fact – yet Jim refused to question, let alone quash, his expectations. As his father was fond of saying, "There's a reason hope rhymes with rope." Jim liked the phrase, and understood it to mean that a little optimism could pull you out of most rough situations.

In the mail was the usual fare: credit card offers, the telephone bill, the cable bill, and the ever-present envelope stamped with bold letters: ***From the Office of J.J. Cross, Attorney at Law***. He opened this one after entering his apartment and dropping the other envelopes onto the bare kitchen floor, which served double duty as a table. Clipped to the legal documents was a handwritten letter on a half-sheet of lined paper:

Jim – I have tried to call, but you refuse to pick up the phone. You leave me no option but to serve these by mail. I only hope that you will not continue to be stubborn. Do what is best for the both of us, as well as for those poor creatures; sign and be done with it, so I can get what belongs to me. Kathy

Her penmanship was unmistakable. Loops that looked like nooses dangled from her *g's*, and her *o's* were as wide and round as the eyes of the fish she was trying to steal. And her word choice was classic Kathy, accepting no blame: "You leave me no option"; "best for the both of us"; "those poor creatures"; "what belongs to me."

That J.J. Cross was now allowing her to paperclip a personal letter to an official correspondence was surprising, but even more surprising was that she had actually bothered to write at all; this proved to Jim that his strategy was having an effect. He shoved the note, along with the legal documents, down among the orange peels and pizza crusts in the garbage can below the sink.

Once he'd removed his boots and dropped them onto the mat beside the door, he noticed that a circle of blood had flowered through his white sock. He sat on the couch, crossed his legs, and removed the sock. On the face of his big toe, just below the nail, was a patch of chalk-white skin, ringed by a narrow band of blood. The dime-sized patch felt like a dry, hardened sponge.

He washed the sore, smeared antibacterial cream over it, and bandaged it. He figured he'd rubbed his toe raw at work, or picked up a fungus from his slippers.

●●●

Seven months earlier, Jim's wife had run away with a fourth-grade teacher. The fact that the fourth-grade teacher was a woman did not make matters easier. He learned of the affair one morning from the woman herself, a sturdy Scandinavian named Blair Gavain who appeared on their doorstep without an umbrella, dripping in the rain, stinking of booze, and swaying on her feet. It was just before nine a.m., and his wife was at school, where Ms. Gavain also would have been, had it been an ordinary day.

She said, "Kathy doesn't love you anymore."

He helped Ms. Gavain into the bathroom. While her face was in the toilet, her hair fell away from the back of her neck, revealing a tattoo of a rainbow being choked with barbed wire. Kathy had only mentioned her on a few occasions, using the same clinical tone she used when discussing other teachers – a tone, he realized once he thought about it, that Kathy employed for most everything, from fudge to funerals.

After vomiting, Ms. Gavain sipped coffee at the kitchen table. She toweled her hair. "Kathy is truly reborn," she said. Her eyes were raccooned with smudged eyeliner, accentuating her pale complexion. She looked ill, although he considered that illness might be her natural state. Some people were like that: robust just one week out of every month, so their health, when it hit, actually seemed like a sickness. "Your wife has hidden her sexuality for two years," she continued, "and she has hidden me for one year. She doesn't want to hide anymore."

"Okay," Jim said.

"She is a different person now."

"So you said."

He stared at the coffee mug – *World's Best Teacher* – in Ms. Gavain's hand, thinking that if Kathy wanted a baby so badly, why turn to another woman?

"You aren't angry?" she said.

He considered this. Should a person be angry after being struck by lightning?

The divorce was speedy, resulting in what he'd thought was an equitable division of assets. He got the truck, she the Accord. They split the money from the sale of the house. Pet custody hadn't been spelled out; she'd ended up with the hamsters, he the fifty-gallon aquarium stocked with tropical fish, which had been a wedding gift from her parents. Her adultery gave him a measure of leverage, but rather than seek more money, he'd taken away her fish. At the time, both parties had been satisfied – legally satisfied, at any rate.

Feeling a grim pleasure, Jim had watched Kathy's lips tighten and her face blush as she read, and then signed, the papers. Her lawyer had undoubtedly advised her not to complain; after all, it could've been much worse.

But she couldn't be silenced forever. When Kathy wanted something, she didn't quit until she got it. Jim had been anxiously anticipating what she might do next.

Now, for the past month, she had been demanding custody of the aquarium, while he had been pretending not to notice.

●●●

One week after the first sore appeared, Jim stood with Boris in the back of a semi, on a local move. Boris unearthed a bureau from its tomb of furniture pads while Jim tossed his sweat-darkened T-shirt toward the mouth of the trailer. Boris asked what had happened to Jim's shoulder, indicating a sore that looked just like the one on Jim's toe: same size, same red ring surrounding a dry white patch.

●●●

Jim's doctor ran a gloved index finger over the sores. He pushed each one as if it were a doorbell. His breath was warm against Jim's neck as he leaned in. "Does this hurt?" he said.

Jim said it didn't.

"I'm prescribing a multivitamin," the doctor said. "If they don't go away in a month, we'll send you to a dermatologist."

●●●

The third and fourth sores appeared after a night of unsettling dreams. Groggy, scratching the base of his scrotum, Jim walked into the bathroom. He urinated, flushed, washed his hands, and then checked himself in the mirror. Two bull's-eyes, one on each cheek, were planted there as if someone had drawn them on while he slept.

He sat heavily onto the toilet. He lowered his head between his legs to fight back a surge of lightheadedness. There had been no warning; there was no reason.

●●●

The guys at work bombarded him with questions.

Jerry wanted to know if the sores itched. He suspected ringworm. Boris thought it looked like eczema. Dwayne untucked his own Best Way Moving and Storage shirt and revealed a scar from a mysterious lesion born on his hip after a night of skinny-dipping in a Malaysian river. The scar was the size and shape of an egg, slightly paler than the rest of his skin.

Soon every man was pulling up his clothing. Willie showed Rottweiler bites on his calf. Beside Ken's spinal cord, a patch of leathery skin stood as a reminder "not to stand with your back to the circus fire-breather." Burt wore a skin bubble on his knee. Matt displayed a fungal growth on his big toe that looked like a wad of gray bubble gum.

●●●

"Maybe I'm just flawed," Jim said to his father, two weeks later. "Or got some new disease that doesn't have a name yet."

"We're all flawed," said his dad, leaning back in the recliner, adjusting his rear end and crossing his ankles. There was a thoughtful expression on his face. He nodded toward the cigarette between Jim's fingers. "Honestly, I had many more health problems when I was drinking and smoking than I do now."

Jim flicked his cigarette with his thumb. He continued doing this even after the dead ashes had fallen away. His father had always been exceptionally good at sounding nonjudgmental while passing judgment. "They have no idea what it is," Jim said, under his breath.

A new sore had appeared on Jim's neck. An allergist had pricked Jim's back with forty-five syringes, loaded with everything from cat urine to beer to Jim's own sweat. No reactions. A dermatologist had ruled out a list of superficial disorders: nummular dermatitis, psoriasis, bedsores, lichen planus, pityriasis rosea. The dermatologist felt "fairly confident" that these were not cancerous bodies, but had cautioned Jim to notify him if the sores changed shape, texture, or color. The next step was to check for neurological abnormalities; Jim would have a CT scan in three days.

"You're probably right about my lifestyle," Jim added. His father also had a way of making things sound simple. And Jim internally conceded that the problem *felt* simple. *Circle of dried skin surrounded by red ring. A skin condition. Simple as that.* Jim felt no physical pain, no anger, no fear, no sadness – only confusion. The sores weren't *doing* anything. They just *were*. Jim finished his beer and then squashed out his cigarette.

●●●

When the CT scan revealed nothing abnormal, Jim quit drinking and smoking.

He spent the first week snapping at his coworkers. Nobody was his friend. At the 44th Street warehouse, Boris took a swing at Jim during a coffee-break euchre game, but missed and threw out his shoulder. Everyone blamed Jim for the injury.

Jim's teeth pulverized gum and destroyed corn chips. He took long nightly walks around the parking lot of his apartment complex. In bed, he dreamed in movie scenes. One night it was Rocky Balboa in gray sweatpants, chasing a chicken. Another night it was *Mad Max*, when the guy chucks a boomerang into the air and it comes back and chops off his own fingers. Jim's motto was Cold Turkey or Nothing. Within three weeks he felt more relaxed, and even discovered that climbing the stairs to his apartment no longer left him winded.

Abstinence wasn't easy, especially with new sores popping up every three or four days. Jim took to watching the tropical fish. It distracted him. The neon tetra and the silver dollar loved to meet face to face behind the green leaves of the peace lily; Jim wondered if they enjoyed gazing into each other's eyes. The checkerboard cichlid spent hours hovering near the bogwood, contemplating, in perfect stillness, the side of the tank. The zebra danio was the athlete, and it zipped relentlessly around the perimeter; fifteen consecutive laps was its record. The tiger barb, a deep green with splashes of Halloween orange, enjoyed nipping the angelfish's tail.

The divorce had squeezed Jim into a one-bedroom apartment, number 197 in a complex of two hundred units. The open kitchen's plentiful countertops were offset by the lack of space for a table, which would have mattered, had Jim still owned a table. Every wall was as white as correction fluid, and the gray carpet emitted a perfumy odor when he vacuumed. The narrow wooden balcony overlooked a lot behind an insurance agency, where businessmen from the nearby paper plant parked their SUVs at odd hours. They didn't care who saw them snorting cocaine off the dashboard.

Drinking was tougher to quit than smoking. Jim slipped one evening and bought a forty-ouncer of King Cobra. An hour later, he returned to the corner store and bought a twelve-pack of PBR, which he polished off in five hours. He needed to get drunk like he needed to breathe, and his rationale in the frenzied moments before cracking that first one was that it was insanity for someone in his condition – a spotted oddity who belonged behind glass – *not* to be drunk whenever possible. He thought about Kathy, and imagined her French-kissing Ms. Gavain. He remembered *Mannequin II* at the Lakeshore Drive-In during their honeymoon in South Haven, Kathy sitting beside him in his pickup, smiling her sizable smile, exposing remnants of Jujubes between her teeth, saying she couldn't stand it anymore, that they needed to move out of Grayling, to a bigger city.

"It's only Grand Rapids," she'd said. "It's only two hours away." She'd produced a note from her purse, written by her parents: *Dear Jim, we know that you and Kathy have roots here, and you will always be welcome, but our daughter, your wife, needs to see the world. Take her where she has to go.*

He'd fought it. They'd grown up in Grayling, had gone to the same high school, the same eye doctor, same gas station, same Long John Silver's...He had a good job at the tool and die shop; she kept busy at the daycare. Why move now? Why move at all? Why why why?

Jim passed out on the couch with his head in a plate of baked beans.

Five days of hangover abstinence followed, and then Jim relapsed again during league bowling. The following day, when two fresh sores appeared in the middle of his forehead, Jim swore to quit drinking for good. He severed himself from situations that would place him in proximity to alcohol, which meant that he bowed out of the Alley Gaterz and stopped socializing with his coworkers. He left his apartment only for necessities. Half of his free time was spent observing his fish, the other half sipping Dr Pepper on the balcony while the classic rock station blared from his boom box. He slapped his arms when mosquitoes lighted there. His television was broken.

•••

Every other day he had a doctor's appointment. He had maxed out his sick time, and now each appointment chiseled into vacation hours. His insurance plan paid 75% for dermatological conditions. The bills poured in. The 25% that comprised his responsibility so far added up to $3,518.49. He maxed out two new credit cards.

Kathy's attorney left frequent phone messages, demanding that Jim sign the papers and release the aquarium to its rightful owner. The attorney claimed to possess sworn statements from the weekend manager of The Pet Emporium, attesting that it was *Kathy* who had come in "Sunday after Sunday after Sunday to purchase fish food," *Kathy* who had inquired about air filters and gravel and vitamin supplements, *Kathy* who showed true affection for the tropical fish, and thus *Kathy* who should be their "guardians."

"I will take this to court, if you force my hand," J.J. Cross threatened. "You have thirty days."

This was Kathy's way. Rather than buy a new aquarium, she would pay an attorney thousands of dollars to bully the fish tank out of his possession. Jim recalled other incidents (recruiting her big brother Tommy to "persuade" Jim to ask her on their first date; Kathy's best friend Jaimy just "happening" to run into Jim at the department store and casually mentioning Kathy's desire for Eternity perfume on her upcoming birthday). When *her way* was what mattered, Kathy would stop at nothing to find someone to get it for her.

And she always knew what she wanted – that is, until she didn't want it any longer. She had once committed to becoming "the best beautician in northern Michigan." Then, after dropping out of cosmetology school, she vowed to get her real estate license. When selling houses didn't pan out, she dreamed of starting her own day care, a plan that never went past reading *Being = Doing: How to Transform Yourself Into a Business Superstar* (another birthday present from Jim, "suggested" by a friend). Kathy eventually finished her college degree and became an elementary teacher, but when she broke into tears only five days after their wedding and said she "absolutely craved" a baby, Jim stood his ground, insisted on condoms, chose to wait her out. He'd gone in fully aware that a marriage was a tug of war, but he hadn't realized that if he pulled hard enough, Kathy would let go of the rope and watch him fall backward onto his ass.

Jim crumpled the legal papers one by one, dropped them into a trash can, doused them with lighter fluid, placed the can on the balcony, and sent the papers into the night sky as a black cloud.

●●●

Jim's relationships with the other movers changed. When they cracked jokes, it was with forced exuberance. They stopped inquiring into his condition, and concealed their own markings. Their concepts of personal space swelled to ridiculous girths. Even when necessity dictated standing side by side – to double-team an entertainment center down a flight of stairs, for example – they pivoted their torsos to create as much distance as possible from Jim. They stored extra gloves in their back pockets so that no man was without, and donned long-sleeved shirts on even the hottest afternoons. During lunch breaks, they peeked at Jim's forehead, where it looked like he had undergone double horn removal.

Jim had never paid much attention to his appearance, but now his face affronted him every day. One doctor prescribed a clear ointment that required exposure to the air, which meant that Jim couldn't wear bandages. His six facial sores (two had recently blossomed on his chin) showed themselves in every reflective surface – the mirror, the toaster, the pots and pans, the sliding glass door of the balcony. He plucked at the sores with his fingers; they were completely without feeling. When Jim ran a fingernail in the red furrows that encircled the hard patches, he felt no pain. It was dead tissue.

Once, Jim leaned toward the mirror, bared his teeth, and growled. When his face contorted, the sores shifted. For a brief, terrible moment, they looked alive and purposeful. The moment passed, and they settled back into position.

His parents visited when they could, driving the 126 miles from Grayling bearing meatloaf, scalloped potatoes, sweet potatoes, spinach, lasagna. They were concerned. Jim's mother touched his face without reservation. Her hand – its eager, unhesitating caress – warmed his skin. Jim caught himself gazing over her shoulder and pitying the tropical fish because they never touched each other, except incidentally.

Dad's latest suggestion was to see a counselor or a priest. A lifelong Catholic, he believed that Jim's condition might be tied to stress caused by a spiritual void. After all, he said, Jim was reaching the age where mortality became a real concern.

"Your mother and I wouldn't be the people we are without faith," he said.

He and Jim were seated in plastic chairs on Jim's balcony, watching the fireflies blink twenty feet below. Jim had stopped attending church shortly after high school, and had no intention of re-enlisting. His father was careful, as usual, not to sound judgmental; he didn't mention Jesus, or any specific god. He disclaimed, "I don't have the answer for everyone, just for myself."

He simply wanted Jim "to keep it in his mind, keep searching for something."

His father claimed to be a living example of "willed healing." He described how, when he was younger – and by younger he meant his thirties and forties – he'd carried an anger inside him. Even though he'd had strong Christian beliefs since boyhood, he had never, as he put it, "let go of myself, completely." His finger circled the rim of his iced tea glass. As if sensing Jim's resistance, he spoke dispassionately, matter-of-factly, trying to downplay the subject's importance. "I realized that this world is going to go on without me, same as it did with me. People possess a certain vanity. I know that when I let go of my anger, which meant letting go of the idea that I was anything more than a servant, my eyesight started improving."

Jim's dad had been born with poor vision. He had a condition called nystagmus that caused his eyeballs to swim uncontrollably in their sockets. They never rested. He hadn't gotten a driver's license until age twenty-six. He had never been able to play any sport that involved a ball. As a teenager, he'd been legally blind.

"Over the past twenty years," Jim's dad said, looking up at the stars, making calculations, "starting about the time you went to high school, my prescriptions have gotten weaker and weaker. I won't ever be 100%, but my glasses aren't as thick anymore."

They sat without talking. Jim strained to hear birds, crickets – any sound of nature – but there was only the drone of traffic on the interstate. All those cars, just one sound. Mother poked her head outside and asked if she could switch on the television. Jim told her it was broken.

●●●

The echoing halls of Northview High, the enormous white teddy bear clutched to the chest of girlfriend number one (fourteen-year-old Kristen Dubrowski, who wore too much makeup and was a devoted Genesis fan), the creek behind St. Jude where Jim and his friends caught garter snakes, Jim's lone Little League home run caused by the right-fielder getting hit in the face with the fly ball...

He could no longer place himself in his own past. His mother showed him photo albums, but no matter how he tried, no matter how explicitly he knew the circumstances surrounding each picture, Jim couldn't make that moppy-haired kid be him. In the mirror, he had stopped seeing himself; he only saw the sores.

Privately, Jim browsed his own photo albums. There was Kathy, humming "She's Always a Woman" as she dried dishes in their new house in Grand Rapids, her face softened by the light pouring through the window. In every photograph, this is what Jim noticed – Kathy's perfect skin, as smooth as a rooftop after a blizzard. She'd always been healthy, never missed a day of work, rarely sneezed, and demonized his smoking. He flipped through the pages, viewing picture after picture, noting her strained smiles, noting how often her gaze pointed down at some unknown spot on the floor, and eventually Jim began to understand that Kathy's health was a symptom of a serious illness; her flawless nature was chronic and debilitating. Being married to someone like him had been an unbearable burden.

Aside from work, Jim spent almost every waking moment on the couch, seated at an angle that prevented him from seeing his reflection in the aquarium glass. He watched the tropical fish do their weightless dance. With each flick of their tails, they seemed to know where they were going, but once they arrived at their destinations, they never did anything. Swim here, swim there. They didn't need purpose; the destination *was* the purpose. As long as they *had* a Point B, they were happy.

The water in the tank, though, became murkier. Jim leaned in close and spotted a filmy membrane grown over the zebra danio's left eye. The deformity didn't appear to be bothering it – it still kept up with the others, and hadn't lost its appetite – but Jim resolved to clean the tank more often.

One day, Jim broke his own rule and adjusted his eyes to view his reflection in the fish tank glass. There were eight sores on his face. More surprising than the number was their arrangement. The sores were divided evenly, almost artistically – four on each half – so that each had a twin.

Jim's body bore twelve additional lesions, which did not follow the mirror-image design of his face. There was no clear pattern. Sores populated the following spots: neck, left shoulder, left elbow, left big toe, left palm, right thigh, right index finger, right forearm, right elbow, right buttock, right pectoral, and one depressing patch on his scrotum. Each night before bed, Jim counted his sores, touching them one by one.

• • •

He survived three counseling sessions. The therapist gave Jim the option of the sofa or the chair. Jim took the sofa. As of late, he'd become fond of studying ceilings.

Ten minutes into the first session, the therapist's deep, delicate whisper lulled Jim to sleep. It was a sudden sleep, pulling him in without warning. He dreamed of an ocean; of soaring over the water; of skimming the surface with the tips of his wings, splashing diamonds into the air. He alighted on the back of a whale and reached into the blowhole; his arm disappeared. The hole turned greedy, sucking at him. He was drawn into darkness.

When he awoke, the therapist was bear-hugging him from behind. Later he said that Jim had sprung from the couch, eyes open, groping blindly and wailing at the top of his lungs. When the therapist attempted to touch him or ask him a question, Jim kicked things – the wastebasket, the chair, the desk, the plants – scratched at the air, and screamed in a barely comprehensible voice, "I won't be swallowed! I won't be swallowed!"

This exact episode repeated itself the next Tuesday, and again the Tuesday following, so Jim and the therapist parted ways. He wished Jim luck, and sent him away with a list of referrals, which Jim promptly stuck to his refrigerator using a magnet photograph of him and Kathy, taken on their wedding day. Whenever Jim retrieved a beer, he could read the phone numbers and names – *Roy Fowler, Psy.D., Emily Greer, Ph.D., ABPP, Yamin Abul, Ph.D., Beckler Foistman, Psy.D., ABPP* – then cast a glance at the wedding photo, like a person peeking through an oven window to see if the pot roast is done.

There were no dramatic outbursts in the priest's office two weeks later. Jim sat in front of the broad mahogany desk, upon which the priest had folded his hands. On the wall behind the priest's head, a golden Jesus observed everything from his golden cross.

"I spent three years in the Philippines," the priest said. "Saw a lot of misery. It won't bother me if you take that off. Whatever's comfortable for you."

"Long as I don't have to see," Jim said. He removed the wool hat and unwrapped the scarf from his face.

The priest didn't flinch. He had white hair and a turkey neck quivering over his collar. He ignored Jim's sores and said without prompting, "I'm getting too rickety to play racquetball." He winced as he stretched his back. "It's a shame. Get old and you start to lose the things you love."

Jim stared at his own hands, which were now spotted with sores.

"No offense, but your breath is...noticeable," the priest continued. "Do you always drink this early?"

"Early doesn't mean the same thing to me as it does to you."

The priest opened a drawer and produced a glass ashtray.

Jim smoked. The priest stood and walked to the bookshelf. He moved his fingers along the spines. He came back to the desk and placed a book in Jim's hands. It was called *Gifts from a Course in Miracles*.

"Pick it up anytime," he said, sitting down. "Look at a verse or two, put it away. I find it beautifully written. Consider it a present, Jim."

Hearing his name spoken aloud, he felt shell-shocked, just as he had with Ms. Gavain.

He held out his hands, showing the priest both sides. He pointed to the sores around his mouth, on his nose, cheeks, forehead, and chin. From his cross, Jesus frowned, pitying the ugliness of the world while doing nothing to stop it. "The doctors can't even find a name for this fucking thing," he said. "Let alone a cure."

The priest reflected. His eyes, as blue as the zebra danio's stripes, appeared to be reading words in the air. "This won't be reassuring," he said, "but the sad fact is that there are mysteries that science can't solve. Sure, they can tell you the physics of what caused this car accident, or the psychological reasons that killer X went into a house and wiped out a family. But other things will always be beyond our knowing. It's the most difficult part of this life. Accepting the idea that we don't *know*. The idea that there will always be things we don't have names for. Things we can't prove. Do we run? Do we feel anger? Of course. Does our anger, our fear, *change* these things? Not in my experience."

The priest wanted to believe that not-knowing was the path to faith. Ignorance was bliss.

"So we accept it, and do nothing," Jim said.

"You got the first part right."

"Just run back to church, act like I believe in something so I can save myself."

"I can't tell you what to do," the priest said, "and I don't recommend impersonating a believer. But even nonbelievers find the services comforting. The ritual of it, I suppose. And you can talk to me anytime." He reached over the desk. Jim gave him his hand. The priest shook it. It was the first time in two months that Jim had touched another human being who wasn't poking or prodding him, and the sensation of the contact halted his breath in his chest. The priest's hand felt dry and leathery, but it was warm, and it was alive, and Jim held it until the priest let go.

●●●

Autumn came, then winter. J.J. Cross's threat of legal recourse after thirty days had amounted to a load of hot air. Phone calls from his office ceased, and shortly thereafter, so did the mailings. Jim was at a loss to explain the sudden shift, but he accepted it without question, choosing to believe it was because Kathy realized she'd been wrong.

The visits from his parents also stopped. Once the initial shock of his sores wore off, they seemed to understand that they were powerless to help. After all, he told himself, his dad had recommended the therapist and the priest, and once these options were exhausted, what more could a father do?

Their most recent visit had been awkward. Mom stood around biting her lip while tears invaded her eyes. Dad stared at the floor with the same expression as Kathy in the photo albums. They also no longer touched him, and Jim understood that despite the doctors' claims to the contrary, his parents had decided, nonverbally, that their son was contagious. They telephoned every few days, but Jim stopped answering; he had nothing more to say; he was no longer their son, he was their *diseased* son, and no amount of talk could change this, just as no amount of counseling or guidance could provide a cure. The copy of *Gifts from a Course in Miracles* lay unread on the carpet beneath his dusty television; the list of psychologists was now confetti on the kitchen floor, scattered like seeds among the pile of unopened bills. The notion that some combination of words, written or spoken, invoked in prayer or in conversation, could erase his deformity...the idea was offensive nonsense, like handing a guy a toothpick and telling him to slay a dragon.

His parents kept their consciences clear by mailing checks for his continued medical treatment. The doctors shaved Jim's head to expose his spotted scalp. Then they shaved the rest of his body – legs, chest, groin, anus, armpits, arms, feet. They wanted to see every last sore, ignoring the fact that each new one was exactly the same as every one prior. Dermatologists prescribed a battery of ointments that succeeded only in making him itch; physicians prescribed pills that made his urine smell like turpentine.

Evidently, word spread that there was a freak up in Michigan who couldn't be fixed: after Jim's doctors tried unsuccessfully to coax him into traveling to other cities to visit with specialists "better equipped to deal with your condition," the specialists themselves flew in, from Cincinnati, Atlanta, Chicago, Minneapolis. They surrounded him, touched him, stuck him, bled him, and proffered mouthful after mouthful of vague, clinical words that added up to nothing. Jim's health – his heart, his reflexes, his blood, his brain – was perfect, and so, before long, the phrase "lesions of unknown origin" dominated the specialists' vocabulary, and they pronounced it with assurance and vigor, as if it were the name of a new baby and they were the proud parents.

Because he never felt physically sick, Jim drank as much as possible. He wanted to possess the sickness – to feel diseased, to feel headaches, cottonmouth, nausea, and stiff joints. He stocked the cupboard with whiskey, rum, vodka, tequila, and wine. Alone in his apartment, he clutched his head. He kicked magazines and newspapers around on the floor. He wanted to justify his horrific appearance by giving himself horrific insides. One by one, he called the guys from the moving company and told them they were shitholes. He harassed Kathy and Ms. Gavain with hang-up calls. With his index finger he touched his tonsils and upchucked in the bathtub so he could examine the horrific insides he'd made. He danced nude in his living room, scratching his sores until they bled, then ran out onto the snow-covered balcony to moon the guys doing lines in the SUV, taking pleasure even when they didn't appear to notice him.

Then, one evening, Kathy called, and Jim answered the phone. It was his first human contact in two weeks. With his blessing, his parents had flown to Italy for a month-long second honeymoon. Despite their eleventh-hour protestations about staying near during this trying time, he'd begged them to take the trip, guaranteeing that the doctors were making progress, that he would be improved by the time they returned. "There's nothing you can do for me," he had assured his father.

When he picked up the phone, Kathy sounded like a stranger, so he treated her accordingly. She wanted to meet for lunch. He declined.

"You don't sound good," she said.

"I'm not good. I'm fucked up."

"I wish you'd meet me."

"You're fucked up."

She sighed. She was probably plucking the telephone cord like it was a bass string. "I wanted to tell you in person, but since you don't apparently *want* that, I'll tell you like this. I don't care about the aquarium anymore. Keep it. Your parents told me about your health problems." She addressed him the way she addressed her naughty students. He understood that he was a naughty student, and that he deserved such a tone.

"These fish are dying," he said, looking at the tank. "I give them food. I clean. But they have tumors and things."

"Jim – "

"The yellow angelfish? Didn't we give him a name? He barely moves. The others want to eat him."

"Jim – "

"I don't know how I should feel about it. He's useless. He barely moves. Maybe they should eat him."

"I've been inseminated, and we're having a baby. I thought you should know," Kathy said. "*I* changed, not you. We have a lot of history together. We shouldn't throw it all away." Even as she spoke, she was swallowing the real substance of her words, releasing only the sounds of them into the air, like the empty, hollow clanks of a hammer on a railroad spike. This was all she could spare, and it was meaningless noise.

He took a moment to assemble a response.

He hung up.

● ● ●

Jim gave up on doctors. The doctors didn't mind; they hated not having an answer.

He no longer went to work. His friends and coworkers stopped calling.

His parents, however, phoned every other day. On the answering machine, they took turns saying they were having a great time, and that they were thinking about extending the honeymoon, but they were concerned about his condition. They implored him to call their villa. If he needed it, they would continue to wire money. They could get back to the States in a heartbeat. No matter what, he was always in their prayers. Each day Jim recorded a new message, assuring them that he was fine ("Actually, I'm feeling really good"), that his condition was improving steadily, albeit slowly, and that he was just too busy with healing to talk right now, but that he would return their call at his earliest opportunity.

The sores covered his entire body, including his ears, eyelids, penis (shaft and head), and the bottoms of his feet. Each had its place; none overlapped, but the edges touched. Long ago, it seemed now, he had given up on tolerating the stares, the confused children breaking into tears, so he never went out. He wrapped his face in his ratty scarf when the Harding's delivery kid brought food, cigarettes, and alcohol.

Each day was devoted to drinking whiskey and watching the quiet, dying fish. A sickness had invaded the tank. The water was clear, but the fish bore signs of disease. The silver dollar floated lopsidedly in place, with a bulbous growth on its left gill. The striped zebra danio, one eyeball distended and filmy, competed weakly for food. A woolly fungus coated the tiger barb's dorsal fin and mouth; it bumped its nose against the glass in a sad, impotent ritual. The angelfish, instead of being devoured as Jim had forecast many weeks ago, had gained a second wind and began nipping aggressively at the other fish, rending chunks of flesh and scales as suited its fancy.

On the couch, hammer in hand, Jim leaned forward. His knee bounced up and down. He looked like a honeycomb; he knew this in spite of the fact that he had thrown away the toaster and the pots and pans, in spite of the fact that he had layered duct tape over the oven handle, refrigerator handle, and faucets, in spite of the fact that he had covered every window, as well as the bathroom mirror, with newspaper. He knew that he looked like a honeycomb because he could see himself in the glass of the fish tank. He was not a man anymore but a design, a puzzle.

His fingers gripped the hammer. His knee bounced. Kathy would never call again – he was sure of this – but she *had* called (hadn't she?) and surely this constituted a victory.

To look at him there, on the couch, his watery eyes darting back and forth, one might believe that he was waiting for just the right moment to leap to his feet, wind up, wield the hammer two-handed, shatter the tank into a thousand pieces, and watch the doomed fish burst free in a rush of water, experiencing for a brief moment the wonderful horror of oxygen.

Acknowledgements

I am indebted to numerous writing teachers through the years: Jaimy Gordon, Stuart Dybek, Elizabeth McCracken, Brock Clarke, Michael Griffith, Rick Moody, and Christine Schutt. To my CMU allies Matthew Roberson, Jeffrey Bean, and Robert Fanning, you inspire me with your outstanding work and your tasteless jokes. My friends Kelcey Parker, Joseph Bates, Alex DeBonis, Sarah Domet, and Darren Defrain gave terrific advice on early drafts of the stories in this collection. For all of the journal editors who were willing to publish these stories, I am forever grateful. Huge thanks to Jerry at Tortoise Books for being such a smart and generous reader. Thanks also to my agent Sara Crowe for continuing to believe in me. And lastly I would like to thank my wife Courtney and sons Simon and Charlie for giving me happiness and purpose.

About the Author

Darrin Doyle has lived in Saginaw, Kalamazoo, Grand Rapids, Cincinnati, Louisville, Osaka (Japan), and Manhattan (Kansas). He has worked as a paperboy, mover, janitor, telemarketer, pizza delivery driver, door-to-door salesman, copy consultant, porn store clerk, freelance writer, and technical writer, among other jobs. After graduating from Western Michigan University with an MFA in fiction, he taught English in Japan for a year. He then realized he wanted to pursue fiction writing and permanently stop doing jobs he didn't love, so he earned his PhD from the University of Cincinnati.

He is the author of the novels *Revenge of the Teacher's Pet: A Love Story* (LSU Press) and *The Girl Who Ate Kalamazoo* (St. Martin's), and the short story collection *The Dark Will End the Dark* (Tortoise Books). His short stories have appeared in *Alaska Quarterly Review*, *Blackbird*, *Harpur Palate*, *Redivider*, *BULL*, and *Puerto del Sol*, among others.

Currently he teaches at Central Michigan University and lives in Mount Pleasant, Michigan with his wife and two sons. His website is www.darrindoyle.com.

About Tortoise Books

Slow and steady wins in the end, but the book industry often focuses on the fast-seller. Tortoise Books is dedicated to finding and promoting quality authors who haven't yet found a niche in the marketplace—writers producing memorable and engaging works that will stand the test of time.

CPSIA information can be obtained
at www.ICGtesting.com
Printed in the USA
JSHW041621010421
13158JS00002B/205

9 780986 092213